A TALE OF A MAASAI GIRL

Naini is not her real name, and some of the details of her life have been altered, but this remains a true account of a girl from the Maasai warrior people of Kenya, who suffered for being a woman, yet triumphed. Naini was raised by two different grandmothers; her difficult and unhappy childhood culminating in the horrifying ritual of female circumcision and marriage at thirteen to a husband who alternately beat her and made her pregnant. Remarkably, Naini overcame adversity, gained an education and her independence. She forged a career in broadcasting in Nairobi, finally leaving Kenya to settle in France. As well as relating Naini's experiences with compassion and a deep understanding, Grace Sicard provides fascinating details of the rich cultural heritage of the Maasai – their customs, ceremonies, dress, stories, medicines, and even riddles. Most importantly she relays Naini's heartfelt and inspiring advice for women who suffer, trapped within traditional societies.

Grace Mesopirr Sicard was born in Kilgoris village in the Narok district of Kenya. She has worked as a scriptwriter, storyteller and announcer for Voice of Kenya radio and television stations in Nairobi. More recently she has appeared in a film on the Kenya Marathon, and in 1995 translated the documentary film *Kasanga* from the Maasai language into French. Currently chairperson of the Kenyan Community and Students Association of France, she now lives in Paris.

A TALE OF A MAASAI GIRL

Grace Mesopirr Sicard

The Book Guild Ltd
Sussex, England

The Book Guild Ltd
25 High Street,
Lewes, Sussex

First published 1998
First published in paperback 1999
Reprinted 1999
© Grace Mesopirr Sicard 1998
Set in Baskerville
Typesetting by Raven Typesetters, Chester
Printed in Great Britain by
Antony Rowe Ltd., Chippenham, Wiltshire

A catalogue record for this book is
available from the British Library

ISBN 1 85776 467 6

CONTENTS

ACKNOWLEDGEMENTS

My sincere gratitude to all those who made my early days in France memorable ones, especially the Lucchini family. Both Mr and Mrs Lucchini played a big part in my success through their tireless efforts in being mindful of my well-being and for providing the necessary assistance, without which the results might have never been the same. Thank you for your kind giving hearts.

I am deeply grateful to my friends and colleagues who generously gave so much of their time and effort in reading the manuscript of this book and making suggestions for its improvement. If I may mention a few: Dr Krisno, Dr Sakaja, Inspector J. Mesopirr, Mr Ngweno, Ole Sankale, Christine and Jacqueline.

Special thanks to my daughter Serah for help in typing, my son-in-law Mr Said, my brother Manuel, for the contribution of some of the riddles, and James Mesopirr.

Finally, I would like to extend my thanks and gratitude through this book to the following whose encouragement and collaboration motivated me to shape my workings: HE Ambassador Karobia and Mr Jones Nzeki, who assisted me in the final stages of my work for correction and rearrangement.

Father Mol's *MAA, A Dictionary of Maasai Language & Folklore* has been of particular help in writing the text.

INTRODUCTION

At the age of 13 Naini was a slender girl of 5 feet 3 inches, innocent-looking and endowed with beautiful black eyes, white teeth with a small gap in the upper front. She was beautiful by any local standard and could have passed for a Maasai tribal beauty contestant. She carried a smile that sent electrical waves of admiration and attraction from the opposite sex, young and elderly.

She was certainly the talk of the village to the extent that her grandmother Nalo-muta, who cared for her, had sleepless nights over what would happen to her future. She would have wished Naini to get married to a young person and enjoy life together. Often in Maasai land, young girls with exceptional beauty found themselves being forced to marry rich and older men.

Thirty years later, Naini still enjoys the same beauty attributes, no wrinkles and a baby face which makes her look 15 years younger. Her tender and electrical smile gives an impression of a person holding the whole world in her hands.

Behind that smile are the immense scars of problems and difficulties that she experienced from the age of 13, when she was forced to be circumcised by the traditions of her tribe, forced to marry at that tender age, had four children, then divorced (broke away).

The story of the life of Naini is full of agony in both body and mind. It is a story that gives a full experience of human torture and the disadvantages of the female sex. It is also a story that reveals to the reader a great deal of the customs and traditions of the Maasai people that exist up to the present, for Naini experienced most of them.

There are many books available in Kenyan bookshops that have been written about the Maasai people's customs. Nevertheless, I feel this real-life experience of child marriage and the upbringing of Naini will bring to light what happens in some communities and hope it will give meaning to the life of those young girls who would otherwise lose the value of their own lives because of depression, when they could have avoided it; courage, hope and self-assurance should play a big role. Where there is a will, there is a way to tackle most of the day-to-day problems. You will understand this from the moving life story of a Maasai girl.

The character referred to in this book is called Naini to avoid mentioning real Maasai tribal names. Based on her personal request, some details of her story are not revealed to avoid a lot of exposure of the characters involved. In order not to invade her family's privacy, various aspects of their lives are not described, but those aspects omitted are not so essential as to make this book incomplete. Perhaps later they will give their permission, perhaps not.

Naini was born into a nomadic Maasai family, some 40 years ago, the first-born of six children. Like both parents, Naini was born in the Rift Valley Province of pure Maasai origin, though they grew up in different parts of Kenya. Neither of her parents went to school, and this is why she wants it put down on paper about her hard-won existence when young, her struggle to bring up her children as a single parent, the hardships she has endured to the point where she is today, even though that is not to her satisfaction. Naini calls on the Maasai people to take education seriously.

Naini firmly believes that if both her parents were educated, she would have had a better life and gained the best that every child could have expected from their parents. If they had had education, they could have perhaps saved her from childhood marriage and guided her to continuing her education till a later time when she could make her independent choice of whom to get married to.

She could have probably carried on with her education until university level or they could have sponsored her to undertake some special training which would have been to her advantage during job-seeking. Today, these are just Naini's thoughts of what might have been; but other obstacles might have cropped up, such as financial difficulties in the family, taking into account the number of children in the home and also the fact that the Maasai during that period did not value or even encourage education in general and especially for girls.

To start from the very beginning, Naini was born an illegitimate child. Her mother, Nariku had fallen in love with a man called Memusi who had intended to take her as a second wife. This was not to be because when Memusi's parents went to formally inform Nariku's parents of their son's intention (in Maasai *apuo enkapti*) permission was denied due to the fact that they claimed that his first wife, King'a Sunye, was related to Nariku (Naini's mother). According to the Maasai beliefs, marriage of two relatives from one home is considered a curse that can bring bad luck into a home. Otherwise her mother would have been married by her biological father had this not been the case.

Naini's mother was later married off to Olomunyak, a distant relative, as a settlement ensuring that Naini and her sister Nareyro remained within the same family. By Maasai tradition, Olomunyak automatically became Naini's father, because of his marriage to her mother. Because Naini was considered the first-born child in the family, he was then referred to by her name, *menye* Naini, meaning father of Naini (direct translation). Naini went on to say this was unfortunate and she feels bitter about it because she could not grow up in the presence of both her parents.

Both her parents are very hard-working. Her mother, to date, still works very hard as she does not believe in getting anything free. Her late father had worked hard, before his death acquiring lots of property and lands bought through his own efforts. While a young boy he worked for other families and when he was a little older he had worked for an English farmer as a milkman, unable to get a better job due to lack of education. When he was young, other people raided their home and took away all their cattle. Through his little earnings he was able to support his mother and brothers and later his wife King'asunye. Naini was born after her two half-brothers from King'asunye had been born.

Naini's mother grew up in a nearby village before she met Memusi. Were it not for the revelation that hindered her mother's marriage to her real father, Naini thinks she could have been much happier. These are of course the thoughts and wishes of a child. Who knows, perhaps life would have been even harder and worse considering that her mother was going to be a second wife. And again, she would have had a lot of half-sisters and brothers. Her late father seemed a kind and good-natured man even though she admits she did not know him very well. She had only met him a few times briefly in the company of his eldest son and daughter, who lived in the same town. There wasn't any closeness between them even though she admired the strong character of her biological father. He was kind to his children although he never gave any support towards her upbringing, even for her education. Once, she had written to him concerning her problems with Tim (her husband). He had written back to her, telling her to first seek assistance from her adoptive father/foster-father and if he didn't help her she should write back and tell him of the outcome. From then on she never wrote to him again. She had expected him to take appropriate action to make up for the past and to protect her, which he never did. Naini felt neglected from both sides, having no one to turn to when she had problems.

Besides that request, she never asked for any assistance financial or otherwise from her biological father Memusi but she had always inwardly hoped and assumed that he would one day ask her if she needed any help. This, unfortunately, never materialised. He is now dead and gone for ever and she wishes she had had a chance to tell him of her feelings held deep inside, and expressed the love and admiration she had for him. By the time of his death, he had over 35 children from three legal wives, excluding Naini and her sister Nareyro.

At the time of his death. Naini had moved to Europe, it had not been possible for her to arrive on schedule for the funeral. All the same, she had sadly travelled the long distance to see him rest in his grave. For the first time, she was so overwhelmed by grief that she wept uncontrollably. She had always wished him well despite her disappointment. This time, she was deeply touched and filled with sorrow. It was then that she realized she had forever lost a loved one, lost the chance of ever being close to her father. This was very painful to bear. She wished she had seen him before his death to make peace with him and ask him to think of her too as a daughter. The reality was difficult to accept but there it was. The great man had departed for ever. Looking at it now, nothing was left in her favour. Maybe he did leave something for her but who will ever tell her this? Surely not her half-brother and her half-sisters. Nevertheless, she misses him dearly. She is sure her late father loved her too but might have been unable to apportion anything to her due to lack of knowledge of legal procedures on how to dispose off his estates equally to his children.

The purpose of writing this book is to put across to the Maa people a word to be vigilant and take education seriously as it is the strongest weapon we can use in this fast-developing world! Naini believes education is the best gift that a parent can offer his/her own children. On the other hand, for those who are in a better position financially, please assist the disabled ones, as one more child offered education is one more Kenyan removed from illiteracy. If each one of us did that, eventually we should have no more illiterate people in our society.

A map of the district showing some of its neighbours

1

BIRTH

Naini grew up in the Maasai village where her mother got married in the company of her adoptive father's brother Lemiso. Ol-omunyak was Naini's adoptive father. Her mother was Nariku. Before being taken to that home where she was going to grow and spend the rest of her childhood, she stayed with her maternal grandmother, *Kokoo*, who was very kind to her and offered all that she could to prevent Naini suffering any malnutrition during her tender years. Naini owed a lot to her. She gave her a good foundation healthwise and, most of all, her love during Naini's entire stay with her for the first five years of her life. It was of course not the same as growing up with one's own mother or parents, but it was the best time she could remember in her childhood. She had good memories of her.

In the Maasai culture, grandmothers are usually assigned children by their daughters or their sons to keep them company in their old age, assist them in the domestic chores and in cases of illness to be sent to call the parents and their doctors for assistance.

This was the case with Naini. She was born and brought up at her maternal grandparents' home as her mother was unmarried then. She had conceived after circumcision. Thereafter, her mother took some leaves of the olmisikioi tree and oseki tree, boiled them in water, added the liquid to milk and then fed Naini with the mixture. She then rubbed some fresh cow-dung onto the back of a cow to signify the first cow given to the newly born baby – *Enkiteng e-nkarna emisigiyioi*, literal translation: the cow of the misigiyioi tree. This cow is usually given by the child's father but since Naini was born at her grandparents' home, they donated the cow.

When Naini's mother got married, Naini was left with her maternal grandparents as was customary. She lived with them until she was five years old before being taken to her adoptive father. Naini thought that her adoptive father cared about her although they always kept a respectable distance between themselves.

The next significant thing that took place after she had been given a name was the removal of her two lower teeth (incisors) when she was between the age of four and five. A child of this age herds lambs and young calves around the home as far as domestic responsibilities are concerned. And between the age of six and seven the tops of both ear lobes are pierced, starting with the right ear, *aud i-nkiyiaa*, using *ol-tidu*, a needle which is put into the fire and when it is red-hot it is then used to pierce through the upper part of the ear lobe, *i-nkitipeta*, then after sterilizing the *ol-tidu* once again, the second ear is pierced. Her second set of teeth was once again extracted *a-abua*. During this stage, a non-school-going child looks after the calves as well as accompanying an older person herding cattle. According to the Maasai tradition piercing of the ear lobes is an important step undertaken during childhood.

As a child, Naini drank milk from her *enkoti* a small gourd, which her grandmother kept for her in the young girl's calabash. Calabashes are used in Maasailand for storing and preserving milk. They must, however, be prepared in a special way for this purpose. After cutting them from their vines, her grandmother would scoop out the insides once they had ripened to remove all the seeds and the poison. She then kept them to dry thoroughly. Once they were dry, she decorated them with beads and cowries *i-saen o sikira* and sewed leather straps using *ol-tidu oo e-mpito*, a native needle and sinew. The straps, made from treated leather, are attached to facilitate the carrying of the calabash. They are also secured around the fingers while milking the cow in order to support the weight of the calabash, and this also protects the calabash from slipping away.

Her grandmother used to clean the calabash for Naini in the early stages but as she grew older, she learnt to clean her own calabash using *esosian*, a piece of stick from the palm tree, together with *i-mbenek oo i-ntulele* (leaves of sodom apple) to scrub the inside and then rinsing it several times with warm water. After drying, it is sterilized using a dry burning piece of olive tree, *oloirien air enkukuri*, before putting in fresh milk. This process is repeated each time after using the calabash. The *olorien* or *ol-tikambu* imparts the characteristic smoky flavour to the fresh milk. This helps the calabash keep the milk fresh for a longer period without getting spoilt, *aisamisu/areku*. Usually before putting the milk into the calabash, a second stick attached to a cow's tail is used to brush out the remaining charcoal from the inside. To date, the Maasai still practise this kind of sterilization to eliminate any germs.

After a woman is married and is blessed to be pregnant, she has to inform two members of the family. First the husband, who should then abstain himself from having sexual relations with her as early as from two to three months of pregnancy and throughout the nine-months period. Sex during pregnancy is unacceptable and considered taboo. It is believed that the child will be unhealthy, as the man's semen will go into the eyes and ears of the unborn baby – in Massai, *aariat enkerai*. If this happens, during the time of delivery the man will be charged to slaughter a goat or sometimes even a cow for the attending women to eat meat. If he refuses, the women gather together, *aanya sogo/olkishuroto*, and slaughter by force.

An expectant woman also informs her mother-in-law, who then alerts the family midwife, *enkaitoyioni*, to follow up the pregnancy, and she will also put the expectant mother on a diet. The *entua* – expectant mother – follows the strict diet pattern until the day of delivery. The *entua* is only allowed one meal per day and milk from a cow which has never suffered from foot-and-mouth disease.

The purpose of giving her one meal a day is to prevent the unborn baby from growing too big in the womb, in case it is not in a good position. The massaging method used to turn the child into a normal position can only work if the foetus was not too big in the womb. The family midwife continues with this exercise on alternate days, even if the baby's head is in the right position, until the day of delivery.

Experienced traditional birth attendants can easily tell the sex of the child by slightly manipulating the lower part of the mother's abdomen and after applying oil and using the natural skills when conducting the clinical check-up during pregnancy until the day of delivery.

Naini's mother Nariku was the eldest child in their family. When she got pregnant her mother became her *enkaitoyioni* and took care of her throughout her pregnancy as she carried Naini. Since there were no clinics, she treated her whenever she was unwell by prescribing some roots and barks of certain trees to boil and drink the juices. As her *enkaitoyioni*, she gave her some exercises and massage to make sure the baby was in a good position. During labour her *enkaitoyioni* was there to deliver the baby, as she has been following up until the very last moment, and to sever the umbilical cord, *osotua le nkerai*. The *enkaitoyioni* was also responsible for burying the placenta or afterbirth *(e-mudong)* after delivery.

Soon after the birth, the child is given *enkarna*, known as *embolet* – pet name – literal translation: the opener. At a later stage, during the ceremony of giving the child a proper name known as *enkarna enchorrio/enkarna emisikioi*, literal translation: the name of the cow's front leg, an elderly lady takes two children aged between eight and ten years old to the river, where they bring water to be used in bathing both the child and the mother. On this occasion, the pet name is examined to see if it is suitable to remain permanently. The decision will depend on how the majority find it. Sometimes, the child may keep the two names. A blessing will then be said, thus *mikitamanya ina arna*: meaning: may that name live with you. The woman and the two children who took part during the naming ceremony, will always remain as part of the family members, eg as godmother.

The Maasai people have no particular way of naming their children. Instead, they would be named after important dead personalities, occasions etc, including names of persons from other tribes. They may also name them in relation to different times and conditions of the day. Listed here are Maasai names and their meanings. Please note that these are literal translations.

MAASAI NAMES FOR BOYS

Kimunyak	–	The one born with luck
Kinyamal	–	The one who gave much difficulties
Ledama	–	Born during the day
Lekakeny	–	Born in the early morning at dawn (sunrise)
Lemayian	–	Born as a result of a blessing
Lemerok	–	One who is not black
Lemiso	–	Born at night
Leparakuo	–	Born of a family rich in every aspect, in cattle, children, wives
Leperès	–	Born while the lands are green
Leshan	–	Born while raining
Leshoo	–	Born while the mother was herding cattle
Leteipa	–	Born in the evening
Nagoroi	–	Named after a dead person, born during the war
Odupoi	–	Successful for getting a child
Oloishuro	–	Born during the *ol-kishuroto* ceremony
Olomunyak	–	A lucky one
Olonana	–	Born when fragile
Olopono	–	Born with a scar on the ear – a child born following a dead child
Oshipai	–	Born when the family was happy, who brought joy

| Parmuat | – | Born at an empty kraal |
| Tobiko | – | Born after long years of waiting |

MAASAI NAMES FOR GIRLS

Kakenya	–	Born in the early hours of the morning
Matishoi	–	Born when drinking
Mayiani	–	The blessed one
Naanyu	–	The one who waited
Naeku	–	Born at daybreak
Naimutie	–	The one who was born late or who was conceived after many years of being barren
Naikuso	–	Born when the mother had worn her best ornaments
Naini	–	The one who is born
Nairesiai	–	Born when the mother was unwell
Naisimoi	–	Born when families of both parents meet often
Naitaari	–	The one given away for adoption
Nalo il-keek	–	The one born when fetching firewood
Nalomuta	–	Born during a journey
Namunyak	–	The one who is lucky
Nanoi	–	Born when her mother was in the midst of sleeping
Napono	–	Born with a scar/mark on the ear or whose ear was cut as a result of a death of another child before her
Nashipai	–	The one who brought joy
Nasieku	–	The one who came quickly
Nemashon	–	Born during a festival
Nenkoitoi	–	Born by the footpath
Noonaishi	–	Born while drinking beer
Nyamalo	–	Born after prolonged labour pains
Paranai	–	Born during a visit
Reteti	–	Named after the *oreteti* tree
Shenana	–	Born when fragile

6

The names given to a newly married lady depends on the circumstances of her arrival at the bridegroom's home:

Ki-lang'u	–	The one who crossed to go to be married (*Ensiankiki natalang'a alo kiyama*)
King'asunye	–	The one who arrived first (*Enkitok edukuya*)
Kitaana	–	The one who came from nearby (*Enkitok nataana enkang' enye*)
Nairuko	–	The one who agreed to be married (*Eiruko pee eyami*)
Nareyio	–	New bride fetched from a far land
Nariku Il-muran	–	The one escorted by warriors (*Il-murran otorikutuo*)
Nariku Nkera	–	The one escorted by children (*Eitairiotie nkera eyami*)
Nashuru	–	The one brought while raining (*Etorikuoki esheita*)
Noolparakuo	–	The one who came from a rich family (*Entito olkarsis*)
Noonkokua	–	Constellation of stars (*Etorikuoki eilepu nkokua*)

There are numerous pet names used by parents for their small children. Other names given to a child are derived from the body parts. Here are some of the names:

Eliyio ai	–	(The one I share lonely moments with) (this is said by a mother to her young one)
Enkiok ai	–	My ear
Enkong'u ai	–	My eyes
Enkoshoke ai	–	My womb My stomach
Esim ai	–	My companion
E-sung'ur ai	–	Mainly said by a woman who has lost many children at birth
Imonyit ainei	–	My intestines (meaning part of me) my entrails

Nana ai	–	My fragile one (girl)
Oi enkutuk e yeyio	–	My mother's mouth
Oloip lai / Enkutuk ai	–	My mouth My shadow
Ostua lai onana	–	My soft umbilical cord My relation

Other pet names used for boys by older ladies and mothers:

Enkeju ai	–	My foot (said by an older lady to a grandchild for running errands)
Nkonyek ainei	–	My eyes (a word mostly used by aged people when requesting favours involving sight)
Osikiria lai	–	My donkey (can be said by a mother to her hard-working son)

The women and the children who participate in the naming ceremony will ever remain close friends of the family.

During the one-month period after giving birth, the mother retains her hair before having it shaved off, occasioning a celebration *in-taleng'o*. The hair kept by the mother after delivery is called *ol-masi*. When the *ol-masi* on the head is shaved, the baby is then brought outside for the first time, after which, she is taken to the kraal and given a heifer. She then rubs some fresh cow dung on the back of the cow; by so doing, it signifies the first cow given to the newly born baby, *en-kiteng enk-arna e-misikioi*, literally the cow of the name of *ene-misikioi* tree.

This cow is usually given by the child's father but since Naini was born at her maternal grandparents' home, they donated her cow.

The shavings were mixed with cow dung and smeared on the calves' pen wall. Generally they are dug into the dung-hill. Naini was then brought back into the hut and given a name.

The name that was given to Naini means the one who has been born. She was named after an elderly lady who was her mother's relative but who died a natural death while her mother was still expecting. Naini was told much later by her mother that her *kokoo* continued to give her some post-natal care, such as treating her whenever she had a cold and during the time she was teething and shaping both her head and the buttocks. This system works very well as one can hardly see a Maasai with crooked legs. This helps the blood circulation and shapes up the newborn's body. She also performed the act of *Ai-rony ilala*, pressing the gum with her thumb or finger to prevent abnormal teeth which often appear from developing.

Naini was brought up in the typical Maasai way of life. Diluted milk was given to her by means of a small horn during the first three months of her existence, supplemented by breastfeeding. Whenever she refused to drink it, her mother would sit behind her, holding her between her legs, Naini's head leaning on her stomach as she was seated on a hide. Cupping her left hand to act like a funnel to Naini's mouth, she then poured the milk from the horn into the cupped hand, and tilted Naini's head back so that the milk was gulped down. Whenever Naini refused to swallow the milk, her mother would hold Naini's nose with her right hand so that she could not breath until she swallowed.

Naini's mother sat not far away from the fire place to wash her. Since there was no tap water, she first warmed the water. After this, she would apply some goat or sheep oil to her body. On sunny days, she bathed her outside the hut after letting the water warm from the sun's heat. She bathed her by sipping a mouthful of water then spitting it slowly, making it look like a running tap.

After delivery, fat is melted for the mother to drink. This fat is made from the tail part of a very fat sheep. Usually the husband is the one to slaughter a fat goat or sheep for the wife and make a dish known as *ol purda* for *entomononi*, (mother) which is a mixture of melted fat and lean meat fried in the fat. For Naini's mother, it was her own family who slaughtered for her as she was unmarried then. Part of the fat was used as baby oil as well as for the mother. Naini, like all other babies, was also fed with fat, which was given in small quantities in order to help the body generate enough heat to keep warm.

The Maasai, both grown-ups and children, dress similarly except for the women. They wear light clothing and it is for this reason that fat is administered and at the same time some of it is applied to the body. The oil drunk by Naini insulated her body from the cold weather to the extent that she could walk in the rain without feeling cold, which is normal for all Maasai children. Even on rainy days, you can see children playing and running around *(ilkongoyek)*.

After delivery, the child is usually breastfed until she/he is nearly four years, by which time the child can walk and is old enough to herd calves around the kraal. During this period of breastfeeding, the nursing mother is usually not supposed to have any sexual relation with the husband, just as when she was pregnant. It is said that if she did so, the child would have a running stomach and this is not acceptable. This measure was and still is practised to space children as the majority of women upcountry do not use modern contraceptives.

The Maasai community staunchly believes that breastfeedings is healthy for both mother and the infant. This is supplemented with milk mixed with juices from certain herbal roots or stripped barks selected specifically for young children.

In the case of an abnormal delivery, e.g. a baby born feet first, there is a ritual to purify both mother and child. This involves slaughtering a sheep and pouring the milk into the placenta. Naini's mother too underwent some of these rituals. She stayed indoors for a full month, during which she was not seen by her boyfriend nor by any other outsiders. Her diet consisted of milk, meat and soup mixed with herbs. She was also given some powder from medicinal leaves to lick, during pregnancy.

If a delivery is normal, a song is sung by some women to alert the men that everything is fine, as the rest take care of the newborn baby after the umbilical cord has been severed. The midwife, *enkaitoyioni*, then asks the mother to kneel down and makes her vomit so that the placenta is pushed out. After this, her stomach is then tied with a wide leather belt (*en-kitati*). The new mother is then given fermented milk mixed with cow's blood. That evening, the rest of the relatives take care of the newborn baby. The following morning the mother is usually given sheep fat to drink.

The women will then remain nursing and feeding the *en-tomononi* for some 30 to 90 days until she is in a position to cook for herself and draw water and fetch firewood. All this time, there are always one or two women attending to her and the newborn baby. These of course are family members, either from the husband's side or the woman's side. In most cases this includes the mother-in-law and the girl's mother. Such ladies are usually older, without the commitments of young ladies with their own young children to care for.

Later, the man will name the child. After delivery, the man will look for a suitable heifer to get blood to be given to the *en-tomononi* after the childbirth. Blood is got from a cow believed to be holy and healthy (*Nasinya*); using a bow and arrow designed for this purpose, they aim at the jugular vein, The blood drawn from each is limited (*ang'oroki en-tomononi*). It is then mixed with milk for her to drink as this is considered as some kind of blood transfusion, because some ladies bleed a lot after delivery, which is usually at home, and the blood and milk is offered as it is believed to be easy to digest. This is also the case for the sick and anyone recovering from an illness. This is still practised.

While living at her maternal grandmother's home, Naini accompanied her grandmother practically everywhere, including going to the forest to dig out some special roots (herbs) used for treating infertile women. Both her grandmothers were some sort of herbalists. Naini recalls that it was her grandmother alone who knew the best proportion of ingredients to mix so as to obtain the full strength of two bitter juices known as *emugutan* and *iseketet* in our village, which were regularly drunk by every member of the family for cleaning the stomach or removing the worms and for treating malaria patients. *Emugutan* was a purgative and after drinking it the patient would feel better and would have a good appetite. Whenever one was unwell and losing weight, the first thing she did was to give the patient *iseketet* just in case it was the worms which were eating his food or rather sucking his blood. If she suspected that a person was suffering from malaria (*oltikana*), she would give *esimeita*. Sometimes, fat from the tail of a sheep or even from other parts of the sheep was also drunk as part of the treatment, especially when one was recovering from illness or after childbirth.

Naini's grandmother also administered some curative herbs from strip-barks, roots devoured from trees and shrubs (*inkabobok o ilkeet, intona,*) which were washed and boiled and the juices drunk as *olmairo*. She also collected some leaves, which she dried and burnt, and the ashes which were by then powder were licked as medication in certain cases. This powder, known as *empunyua*, was also used to treat wounds by applying it on top. Some of these ashes were also sewn inside small pieces of skin and worn as amulets by small children either on the neck or on the waist to ward off evil. Her grandmother most of the time administered the *empunyua* to pregnant women. The one put inside the sheep's or goat's skin for children is known as *in-taleng'o*.

In later life, Naini regretted that she could not remember the exact roots as she was too young to identify them except for *emugutan, iseketet* and *e-simeita* because these were used frequently. *E-simeita* is mainly used to induce vomiting, *alop-ishore* when one is suffering from malaria. The other two are also commonly used when one is attacked by *en-cuka* (worms).

Naini drank the juices of herbs during her youth as they were several times administered to her by her grandmother, and later in life after childbirth. Youths are warned against *en-cuka*, that should they happen to get them or see them in their stools, they should not feel ashamed of this but report to their parents, so that they get treated immediately.

One time, her grandmother had a bundle of four different kinds of herbs. She squeezed them out to get the water from the boiled leaves and mixed them up together for Ole Saidim to drink, who had had an accident.

There was also another incident of a man who was kicked

by a cow in another village. He became so sick that her maternal grandmother was called in to treat him. She asked Naini to accompany her. In this particular case she had first cut three small notches (*ilg'amat okuni*) on the swollen part. The notches were spread around the area to be treated in order to bleed it, using *ol-murunya* (razor) then in turn by use of a horn, *e-mou*, which had been sliced equally all round on the large part. The horn was placed on the very spot where the notches had been made. She then sucked the horn on the top part through the small hole which she had made by slicing off the tip, which was now easily closed to promote or induce pressure. She kept on sucking until she felt that blood was close enough, then she covered the small hole on the horn with a honeycomb (*enk-orong'o*) which she had removed from a beehive (*e-kidong* or *e-mulug*). To determine if there was blood in the horn, it was struck gently. She curled the index finger of her right hand beneath the first fold of her thumb, then with a forward flick, she hit gently at the tip of the horn with her fingernail several times. If there was no sound, then the horn was filled with blood. Then the horn was pierced, using a traditional needle aimed at the honeycomb.

Naini's grandmother repeated it once again after wiping off the blood with some soft leaves known as *i-masilig*. She then put back the horn once again onto the wounded area and then sucked out the air.

After this exercise, she then cut *en-tulelei* fruit into four equal pieces and rubbed it on the spot where she had earlier put the notches. From henceforth the swelling gradually went down. Usually, mainly swellings or chest problems and any dislocation are treated in this way.

The man then continued with his treatment, taking soup (*i-motori*) made from bones and cow hooves (*i-loilelek*), which were first scorched (*a-isui*), to remove the hair then mixed with roots such as *ol-kitolosua*. The mixture was believed to bring about quick recovery. The bones and hooves and the roots were later removed after they had been boiled, and the soup was whipped thoroughly, using a wooden implement called a *ol-kipirre*, which is also used by the Maasai as a means to whip thick milk until it is frothy.

As a child, while at her paternal grandmother's home Naini saw her treating many people in the neighbourhood. She had great skills in this field as she was rewarded many times by her patients, both men and women. As a circumcisor, as a medicine woman in treating barren women to obtain children and delivery, she was well known in her village and the neighbourhood. In fact, she was the one who circumcised Naini and four other girls in the village.

Listed on the following pages are some of the trees and their names she learnt from her grandmother. Scientific names are from Father Mol's MAA Dictionary.

She used trees frequently for medicinal purposes; either leaves, barks or roots are boiled and cooked. Leaves are also burnt to get ashes, which are licked for medicinal purposes (in Kimaasai *empunyua*).

KIMAASAI/ENGLISH SCIENTIFIC NAMES OF TREES AND THEIR PURPOSE

Endamiyie	:	Used for ceremonial purposes
Emugutan	:	*Alibizzia anthelminthica* (used against worms and malaria)
Enkairamiami	:	Used for medicinal purposes
Esimeita	:	Used to induce vomiting in treatment of malaria
Esosian	:	Reed, stick of a palm tree – used for cleaning calabashes
Iseketet	:	Used to eradicate worms
Intulele	:	Sodom apple or thistle used for medicinal purposes, while the leaves are used with esosian to clean calabashes

14

Olchurai	:	Acacia tree (robust)
Ol-darpoi	:	Sausage tree, *Kigelia africana*
Ol-aimuriaki	:	Jasmin (wild fruits)
Oleleshwa	:	*Tarchonanthus camphoratus*
Olerai	:	Acacia tree (*albida*)
Olg'aboli	:	Fig tree, *Fiscus sycomorus*
Olg'ilai	:	*Teclear unifoliolata*
Ol-masiligi	:	Sapling plant – used for medicinal purposes
Ol-morijoi	:	*Acokanthera schimperi*
Ol-misikioi	:	Eaten as fruits and used for ceremonies
Ol-musalala	:	Ventricosum
Ol-kilenyia	:	Roots used for medicinal purposes
Ol-kinyei	:	Maba tree (used together with iseketet against worms)
Ol-kitoloswa	:	Boiled with soup and drunk as a health drink
Ol-oisesai	:	*Osyris tenuifolia*
Ol-oilei	:	*Zizyphis mucronata*
O-loirien	:	Wild olive tree used to impart smoke into a calabash before putting fresh milk into it
Ol-piron	:	Doun palm tree (*hyphaene thebaica*) used during ceremonies
Ol-popongi	:	Euphorbia tree – used by children to decorate their skins
Ol-tarakwai	:	*Juniperus procera* (used for building)

Ol-tepesi	:	Acacia tree (*Seyai*)
Ol-tiani	:	Bamboo, *arundianaria alpina* (small ones used as drinking straws and large ones as boxes to keep and protect poisoned arrows)
Oreteti	:	Rain tree (*Maesa lanceolata*)
Oseki	:	*Cordia ovalis*
O-sinandei	:	*Popducarpus milanjianus* (creeper plant used during ceremonies)
O-sojoi	:	*Eucleau fructuosa* (medicine)
O-sokoni	:	Cassia tree (medicine)

2

STORIES OF THE MAASAI

After the age of five just after the birth of her sister, Naini was taken to her other grandmother (father's side) who was also as kind as her previous grandmother. Although it took her time to get to know the people of that home, she soon adapted to her new surrounding as she acquired new friends. Every evening, her new grandmother told her and the other children of the village some late-night stories which she narrated in turn until they fell asleep.

Here are a few of her grandmother's late-night stories, which always started off like this:

THE STORY OF TUTA

Tuta was born in a village somewhere in Maasailand. When he was born, the same day a girl was born named Sayei in the same village. The two families were good friends, even though they were not from the same clan. The two families were well known for their wealth and large families (*ilparakuo*).

They had lived together in the same village for about seven years. Due to a famine, they had to split and go in different directions in search of greener pastures for their animals. It was dry all over.

The two children had grown up to be good friends too, and they were sad to learn from their parents that they were going to part. The two were good playmates. Tuta had told

17

Sayei, 'I shall marry you when we shall be old enough,' and she had agreed. Before parting due to the above reasons, they had both burst a bead (*aadany osaei tempolos*) in the middle for their engagement and each swallowed a piece as a sign of their commitment to one another, swearing never to marry anyone else. Soon after, they parted. This was their secret and none of the families knew what had transpired between the two. They were young but the promise lasted for many years after.

Years passed by and now both of them had grown big. Tuta was now circumcised and so was Sayei. All this time there was no correspondence between them. Tuta's family went in search for a wife for him, and each time he chased them away. His mother got very worried about this and kept on telling him that he was now a man and he should get married. In turn, Tuta never replied to her and he never told her why. The whole family was concerned about this, except for his father. He told him to take his time and when he felt he was ready to marry, to let him know. He also told him to make his own decision.

Far away in another part of the country, Osayei was sad and longed to see Tuta. She prayed and hoped that one day their childhood promise would come true. Now that she was no longer a girl but a young woman (*esiankiki*), she looked forward for Tuta. She longed to be together with a man who meant a lot to her.

Tuta was *ol-parakuoni* – he was a rich man by now and was well known for his wealth (*karrisisho*) and his generosity to the poor and above all for his handsomeness, and so was Osayei. He was now independent from his family.

One day, Osayei told her mother that she was going to look for Tuta as no other man in the world would marry her, and that she was already engaged to him; seven years before when Tuta left they had burst a bead. Her mother told her, 'My daughter, relax, perhaps Tuta is already married after all these years.' 'No! no!' she cried, '(*a-a yeyioo*), no mother, I know him well he cannot do such a thing. We belong to one another I am sure he is still waiting for me!' she said. No one in the family had managed to persuade her into marriage with somebody else.

She then requested her family to slaughter a sheep for her and make *ol purda* for her and put it into a container (*olnoos*) for her long journey. She had also requested two calabashes of milk to carry along with her.

Next morning, she woke up and bade everybody farewell and left in search of her lover. The journey was hard and long, above all because she didn't know where to start. She walked throughout the day and at sunset she climbed to the top of a tree and tied herself onto it in order to protect herself from falling off.

That night, she heard a lion roar, then in response, she replied, '*eidiirro eidiirro olosiria to-loilei kake mapal Tuta lo Sayei le meiting aalo*. It has roared the one of Isiria in the *Oloi lei: zizyphus mucronata* but I cannot stop the search of Tuta of the bead without end ... I am going.' Then after that she slept.

The following day she started walking early in the morning and in the night she climbed a tree again, just as the previous night. That night the lion roared again and she continued to reply as the previous night. This went on and on for six days. Each night she heard the lion roar and continued to reply as before. Each evening she ate *ol purda* and now she was beginning to run short of food.

She was now worried of what would happen to her if she did not find Tuta. In the night she again heard the same lion. Now she began to believe that the lion was guiding her in the right direction. She also believed that the same lion was there to protect her. Throughout her long journey she never encountered any problems.

One morning she got up early as before and walked for a while. Then she heard some noise, and stopped abruptly. She could now hear the cow bells tinkling from a distance. She was excited and full of hope that she had at last found other people after so many days of travelling, and looked forward to arriving at her destination. She noticed many herds of cattle. She kept on walking, and on approaching, she saw a young boy herding the lot, and asked him, '*I-nkuneng'ai kuna kishu?*' (Whose cows are these?)

The herd-boy answered, '*Ine Tuta*' (They belong to Tuta).

'*Oo kunda?*' And those ones?

'*Ine Tuta.*' They also belong to Tuta.

Herds and herds – she could hardly count them now.

She waited until sunset and then accompanied the cattle with the herd-boy. On the way, there was a river and she waited until the boy had crossed the river, then she cried out for him to come and take her across. The boy was afraid of her because of her outfit because she was dressed in monkey's skins. He was not sure if she was actually human. He could only see her eyes through the holes in the skin. He could also see her nose and mouth – everywhere else was covered.

She insisted that he return for her. She said, 'Please come and fetch me.'

Sayei told the boy to spit across the river and if it touched her between her bosoms then she would cross alone. The boy did as he was told but he failed the first time and on the second trial it hit between her bosoms. The girl then did the same thing and had to cross alone.

When they arrived at Tuta's home, the boy invited her to his mother's hut in the village. Apparently this boy was Tuta's brother! He introduced her to his mother as *entiamasi ai* (legendary animal), and his mother was astonished.

'Why should you bring *entiamasi* to our home,' she asked?

The boy said, 'Because she wishes to see Tuta!'

'Oh my God!' cried the mother, 'and you dared bring her knowing how Tuta is! You know Tuta is going to kill her. If he can chase all the beautiful girls of the land, what makes you think that he will want to see this one?'

'He must and if he says no, then I shall keep her for myself. She is mine,' the little boy continued. 'I found her and she will stay with me here at home.'

The mother could not argue with him any more. She agreed with him.

Sayei was surprised that there was plenty of grass in this

region, unlike where she came from, which had experienced a lot of drought. Later that evening, she came into *emboo oo nkishu* just to admire Tuta's cows chewing their cud (*Eny'aal ingamuran*) while they were being milked.

That evening, Sayei was sitting outside watching the family going on with *eramatare* (milking the cows etc.) when all of a sudden she heard once more the lion roaring in the nearby forest and she acknowledged as before.

They were all surprised to hear her reply to the lion. Tuta's mother thought the lady was crazy as she could not understand how she could talk to animals. After that they had gone into the hut and they all ate together then she was shown a place to sleep.

The following morning she accompanied the herd-boy to look after the cattle. Later that afternoon, she asked him about a place suitable to take a shower in the river. The boy was curious to find out what kind of animal this was who could talk and walk on two legs! He then followed her secretly without her knowledge and hid to watch her from a distance. She went into the river after removing all her monkey-skin clothes and washed, and after that she dressed. The little boy could not believe his eyes! He saw that she was very beautiful indeed. He was glad that she was not an animal but a beautiful young lady. All this he kept to himself as he did not want anyone else to know because Tuta might get angry with him later if he learnt of his spying on the girl.

That evening, Tuta returned from his trip and his mother briefed him of the arrival of the *entiamasi* and the wish of his younger brother to keep her. Just like the previous days, the lion roared again and she in turn replied as before, to his disbelief. Tuta wished she could sing once again but she never did!

The third day, she accompanied the boy as the other days. She went to have a wash as usual, unaware of the presence of Tuta and the boy watching her from a distance. Tuta could not believe his eyes. 'If it is true,' he said to the little boy, 'then she is the woman I have been waiting for!'

21

His brother was now rejoicing at this news. He too hoped it would be as his brother desired.

That evening Tuta had asked his brother to go to his hut after dinner with his 'legendary animal' (*entiamasi*). The boy agreed and went there with her that evening. Tuta's hut was mudded and the roof thatched with grass. Tuta then started to interrogate Sayei and she told him everything from the very beginning: that they used to herd cows together and they had promised to marry. That they had broke a bead in the middle and each swallowed a piece as a promise to one another.

She asked, 'Is it Tuta or a mere resemblance? I cannot believe my eyes.'

Tuta insisted that she should remove the monkey's skins she was wearing and at last she agreed. Then he said to her, 'I knew from your youth days that you would turn into a beautiful woman.'

Osayei reflected that she had wept bitterly when Tuta and his family had to go far away in search of water and green pastures for their herds of cattle.

The fire glowed as Tuta and Sayei sat facing each other in his *osinkira*. They both felt strongly for each other and they both remembered their childhood together in *osupuko* (the highlands) before Tuta's family left for greener pastures. They were then young and hot-blooded and as they both looked at each other in the dim firelight, their hearts beat faster with love for each other, after a long time of separation.

They moved forwards so as to be closer to each other as if pulled by the force of gravity, and their emotion was great. Tuta then told her his part of the story, that he was given at least four wives of which he had said no to all of them just to wait for her! All this he had done in order to keep his promise as they belonged to each other. Tuta's younger brother was there to encourage the young maiden in order to promote her achievements.

The following day, the news spread very fast and the wedding was arranged and they married without further ceremonies and lived happily together thereafter with lots of children.

The End – *Ne-iting' eba neija*

This story was told to serve as an example of one keeping his/her promise on what has been agreed upon.

THE STORY OF OL-KURRUK THE HYENA AND A MAN

Once upon a time there was a man who went to visit his in-laws who lived a long way from their own village. When he arrived there, (*neinos il-omon*) then they exchanged news. He stayed there the whole afternoon and was then given *en-tawuo* – a young heifer. He then tied a rope around its neck so as to be able to lead it to his home.

It was a long distance. On the way before sunset, he stopped to eat some *ilamuriak* fruits. Meanwhile he had tied the heifer to a nearby tree while he went round to eat the fruits, round the cluster of trees (*o-sanang*). The *o-sanang* was so large that by the time he went round, it was very late in the night. On going to where he had left the heifer, he got hold of a hyena who was trying to escape. 'Ah! so you have cut the rope!' He removed the rope from the tree and put it round the hyena's neck and continued on his journey.

When he arrived home, his wife screamed with terror. 'How can you bring a hyena home!'

The husband got so furious because of this remark. 'How dare you say a thing like that! My *pa-ashe* gave me this heifer which she had promised sometime back and you dare say this? Shut up or I shall hit you, if you continue saying this.'

The wife was shocked to notice that her husband could not make out the difference between a hyena and a heifer! The husband didn't realise that he had stayed so long in the forest that evening and the hyena had eaten the heifer. She left her husband at *olale loo lasho* – the calves' pen – and then entered the fire place, which was also their bedroom, and sat on the bed. She was in deep thought and was still shaking because of the hyena. After a few minutes, he also followed

23

her. He then went on to give her the news of her parents and of the fruits he ate on the way.

In the meantime, the hyena had killed one of the calves at the *olale* and the rest were now running up and down, too afraid! She went to check what was happening. The wife told him that one of the calves had been killed by the heifer (hyena, but she was afraid to mention that name) and that he should do something about it. He then took *ol-ng'oret* – a blocked arrow which is used normally for bleeding cows by piercing the jugular vein to draw blood. He then got hold of the hyena's neck and tied it with a rope and then drew blood. He filled a calabash then afterwards he untied the rope and sat down to drink the blood. He tied the hyena at the corner away from the calves in the calves' pen.

After that, all was calm. He offered his wife some blood but she rejected it. Her husband went to sleep. As for his wife, she couldn't sleep because she was afraid that the hyena might cut the rope to escape and probably come and kill them! Soon after, the husband started to complain of stomach-ache. He then told his wife to move away so as to allow room for his protruding stomach until there was no room for her in bed to sleep. His stomach was swelling every few minutes like a balloon being filled with air. By now he was nearly bursting and could hardly breath. He told his wife to break the wall (*tuputo ena suntai*) so that his stomach could pro-trude through the broken wall. By now he could not speak.

The wife then rushed to call the neighbours to come and kill the hyena. They all came into the house. On seeing the hyena, they were all terrified at the sight. They then untied it and pulled it outside and speared it to death.

Meanwhile the man had blocked his anus so as not to fart or excrete inside the house, using a piece of soft leather. At dawn, they carried him out of the village and placed him where the ground was high, his bottom facing the lower part of the ground. Until that moment no one had realised that he had put *empising'iet enemodiok pee merot aashu ninye ashik* into his anus to prevent himself from excreting or even fart-ing. His whole body by now was swollen to the extent that one could only see the sockets of his eyes! They had no more hope that he was going to live. They were just waiting for him to die any moment now. While they were still standing there wondering what to do to save his life *ol-kurruk* – a crow – came singing hop-hoping towards this disabled man. Hop, hop, *kurruk, kurruk* and with his bill, he removed the bung from the man's anus! Since they had laid him in the sloping place, his fluid excreta (*enkoroti*) made a big pool (*olturoto*). Then the man's stomach went down like a balloon after releasing air, and as he filled the pool, he kept on saying *ol-kurruk tabaa i-lewas'* repeatedly – literal translation: crow cure the men – crow cure men!

As for the crow, he never got a chance to fly away. He was blown away by the strong force of the sudden gushing flow of the fluid excreta. He was buried there and never saw the sun again as he died, but saved the greedy man's life.

The End – *Ne-iting' eba neija*

This story was told to the children to listen to their parents as disobedience and carelessness can cause one a lot of shame. Referring to the story of this greedy man, if he listened to his wife he would not have suffered the way he did.

THE STORY OF KITASIOYIA

Once upon a time, a lady gave birth to an *entiemasi*, a monster with a human face but in fact it was a cannibal. The first day after it was born, the father slaughtered a goat for *entomononi*. The ladies of the village cooked plenty of the meat in a big clay pot. They had put on a lot of firewood and left to do other duties.

Kitasioyia and her mother were fast asleep. When Kitasioyia woke up, she smelt the cooking. Leaving her mother in bed, she crawled and collected a big spoon to scoop the meat. She ate it so quickly that it burnt her mouth. After eating, she returned the bones to the pot and went back to sleep beside her mother. The mother didn't hear anything as she was completely tired.

When the other ladies returned to the house, they continued adding firewood. They didn't suspect anything sinister. When Kitasioyia's grandmother came, she was hungry and she removed a piece of meat to test if it was already well cooked. To her astonishment, there was practically no meat in the pot, only bones. She was shocked, and to her disbelief, she called another lady to double-check. The second one also confirmed that there was no meat.

At this point, they woke up Kitasioyia's mother, to ask her if she had eaten the meat. Up to this point, nobody suspected anything. They then removed the remains of the meat and threw away the bones. They again filled the pot with meat. This time, they were determined to find out about the mysterious disappearance of the first meat. By then Kitasioyia was sleeping.

After lighting the fire once again, they set the pot into the fire. They had then told Kitasioyia's mother to follow them outside, leaving the baby on the bed. While outside, the ladies talked secretly amongst themselves, back biting about Kitasioyia even though they hadn't any concrete grounds to suspect her. One thing they were sure of was something was wrong with the new-born baby. They had tried to feed it, but it couldn't breast feed nor drink the diluted milk. On checking its stomach, it was too big. The child was constipated – *epong'a*. This was a puzzle, and they were yet to find out. The mother was then advised to keep a close watch of its movements and of every abnormality that might occur during the time they were sleeping.

No sooner had she gone back to bed and pretended to be fast asleep, than a strange thing happened. Kitasioyia woke up and crawled to the fire place and opened the pot! Then she murmured something to herself several times. Then all of a sudden she said aloud, '*Kurtet ti-nyikinyiku, enk-alem tinyikinyiku*' (direct translation – spoon draw near to me, knife draw near to me.) The mother nearly fainted from what she saw and from what she had just heard! Kitasioyia then

26

started eating all the meat as fast as she could. After that, she put back the bones and some lumps of soil from the temporary wall, and covered the pot once again – then crawled back to bed and lay beside her mother without disturbing her. When the mother saw her climbing the bed, her heart leapt and nearly stopped with fear, but she had to be strong not to scream and not to show any tell-tale signs to betray herself that she knew anything and not to alarm Kitasioyia. For some seconds, her mind was blank and she couldn't figure out what to do to her poor child. It was difficult to decide whether to tell the rest of her findings, as she had no intentions of harming the child. It didn't harm her during her pregnancy and so she had no intention of destroying it after carrying it for nine months. But then she must do something about it. With this in mind, she woke up quietly, went outside and called the rest. She then secretively conveyed her findings about Kitasioyia. They then conspired, planning how they would get rid of Kitasioyia. Everyone was informed in the village and a solution was arrived at. Kitasioyia's mother went back to bed not to provoke any suspicious feeling.

While she was in bed, the rest arranged to boil all the fat – *aashol isunya* – and later added it with milk and gave it to Kitasioyia to drink. She drank it all and after a while, she was fast asleep. On seeing this, the mother woke up quickly, packed her belongings and left with the rest of the family. Before leaving the village, they tied a donkey and a goat in the *olale* in the same hut and closed the door with *orike*.

When Kitasioyia woke up in the early hours of the following day, just after the first cockcrow, she didn't realize that she was alone. The door was closed, the fire was out but the pot was still on the fire place. She started crying as she had done the previous day, but no one came. As she continued crying she realized that something was wrong. There was no movement. She looked for her mother but she wasn't there. All of a sudden, she heard a movement. She asked, 'Are you there, mama?' No one answered. 'Ah!' she exclaimed, 'you thought you were going to abandon me. You cannot leave me!' But when she moved closer, because it was still dark at the *olale*,

27

she was shocked to see that there was just a goat and a donkey. On checking again she realized that everyone had left.

She opened the door and went outside, only to find out that the village was empty. There were no cows, no people and the *enkishomi* was ajar. With disappointment, she returned to her parents' hut and closed the door with *orike*. She lit the fire; by now, she was angry that she had been cheated. She opened the pot (*emoti*) and picked out the meat, ate and then went back to sleep. The oil she had drunk the previous day had some effect on her. She had a running stomach and was feeling weak. What was she going to do now? She decided to go back to bed and sleep until sunrise. In the morning, she was still feeling tired. By evening, she thought of what she was going to do with the goat and the donkey left behind. She untied the goat and drove it outside. By now she was once again feeling hungry and she sat down to think of what to do. She wanted to eat some meat from the goat, but how? She wondered how she would do it without a knife to slaughter it. What must she do now?

Then an idea cropped up. She could go through into the stomach of the goat through the anus *en-e-modiok* then she could eat all the inside parts of the goat; the liver, kidneys, intestines and the heart. And that was what she did. Kitasioyia ate all the entrails of the animal after entering into the stomach through the anus. Before the goat died, she heard people talking, saying they would drive away the goat and the donkey. To this end she had answered them immediately inside the goat's stomach. '*Entapal enkine ai, o sikiria lai*': Leave my goat and my donkey alone.

They were very shocked to hear this and when they looked around they did not see anyone. They ran as fast as their feet could carry them. They thought it was the goat that spoke. At last the poor goat fell on the ground and died instantly. Kitasioyia then came out, satisfied from her own acts. Oh! she said, it was very hot in there. She had to stay overnight at the old empty homestead. She then took the donkey into the house and closed the door with *orike*.

That night, Kitasioyia heard hyenas laughing and making

28

a lot of noise around the spot where she had left the remains of the goat earlier on in the day. She was now afraid and wondered what she would do next once she had cleared the donkey. The following day she woke up early took her donkey and left the village, heading to an unknown destination. She had no idea where she was going. She did the same thing to the donkey, entered into the stomach once again. It took a little more than four days as the donkey was bigger than the goat. She had practically a whole week of feasting, including of course the goat she had eaten the day of her birth, which was meant to be for the mother and the ladies who had come to assist during delivery and the feeling of *entomononi* and prepare *ol purda*.

She started walking until she could walk no more. She managed to get to a nearby river bank and drank a lot of water and sat there to wait for its prey. The river was deep and wide and she couldn't cross on her own. As time went by her hopes diminished as there was no sign of any human being to come to her rescue.

Later that afternoon a miracle happened. She heard people talking as they approached the river. She was so excited and her mind was now busy working on what she was going to do next. She must act quickly, now or never. She sat there waiting patiently. There were warriors going on a hunting raid trip, *il-murran oo puo en-jore*. She greeted them, '*Entasopa lo murran.*' The warriors were amazed, they couldn't believe their ears! After that she requested the first one to help her cross the river but he refused. The second and the third did the same but she never lost hope. To her surprise, when the last one came he agreed. The others told him not to accept because it was a devil: *esetan!* They went on to tell him, 'If it was a real child then it could not be talking,' but he never listened to their advice.

He said, 'The little thing is in trouble. I cannot leave a helpless thing to die when I am able to help' (*nenya emodet*). Ole Melita didn't listen, he went out of his way to pick up Kitasioyia. As soon as he did, he realized his mistake and the problem he had put onto himself.

After crossing the river, he asked Kitasioyia to come down but Kitasioyia asked him to carry her just a little further as she was very tired. She continued to beg, 'Please just until that tall tree,' on and on until she had dug her claws deep into Ole Melita's back. By the time Ole Melita reached the tall tree Kitasioyia had already dug all her claws into the warrior's shoulders and hips. He told her to come down after arriving at the agreed spot, but she just laughed at him! 'I am not coming off your back,' she told him, 'so keep walking because I am not leaving you alone!'

Ole Melita was surprised. He tried to shake her off from his back but all was in vain. He was shocked and ashamed of what he had done. He now wished he had listened to the others. It was too late now as he was going to carry her for several days. He had lost the whereabouts of his colleagues due to his own stupidity in agreeing to assist this little devil. He had lost respect from his colleagues. How would he ever explain this to the elders of their village? He regretted it very much.

Day after day he kept wandering all over the forest. He was afraid to fall asleep as he thought Kitasioyia would eat him in the night. On the other hand he was afraid to go near his home in fear that Kitasioyia might eat all the people of his village. This he had decided to face alone until he found a solution.

One night (after many nights of wandering and hunger) Ole Melita tried to steal a goat, but when he caught it, Kitasioyia screamed to alert the owners. She cried aloud, '*auui, loorere enyioto amu ewaki ntare inyi*' – meaning: Help! Wake up! wake up! somebody has stolen your sheep! Ole Melita had let go the goat as he was sure he would be caught if he took it because he couldn't run fast with Kitasioyia on his back.

The second night he tried to do the same thing and Kitasioyia once again screamed. Ole Melita was so angry with Kitasioyia that he asked her, 'Why do you act like this? Are you not hungry after all these days? Don't you want to eat?'

Kitasioyia was surprised, then answered, 'I thought you would eat alone without me.'

'No! no!' said Ole Melita. 'In fact I was worried about you. You are so young to go without food for all these days. This is why I wanted to steal the goat, so that we can eat meat.'

'Ah! If this is the case, then I shall keep quiet tonight. I shall not scream again,' said Kitasioyia.

That night, Ole Melita had managed to steal a sheep and carried it far from its home. He went and slaughtered it the same night. He then kindled a fire by rubbing sticks together (*olpiron – aipiro enkima*) and roasted the meat. The warrior melted all the fat and gave it to Kitasioyia to drink. Kitasioyia ate some meat too and was very happy as she was actually very hungry.

Ole Melita made sure that he had given her all the fat meat, including the sheep's tail, which was very fatty. In the back of his mind, Ole Melita was hoping that a miracle would happen to save him from the legendary animal (*en tiamasi*). He had prayed to the God of his ancestors to save him from this *esetan*.

It didn't take long before Kitasioyia started to doze off because of the fatigue and also due to sleepless nights. It was also due to the good meal she had just eaten. When he realized this, his mind worked fast. He would lie down too so that Kitasioyia would not know when he left. He had packed all that he needed for his long journey home if he succeeded in getting rid of her. He had done all that so as not to waste time later.

He added more firewood to the blaze of fire in order to chase away wild animals which might be tempted to come because of the smell of the slaughtered sheep. Slowly he felt Kitasioyia's claws easing their grip, slowly until all were completely out. She was now on the ground. He quickly picked up his sword, spear and the meat he had packed earlier for his trip. He then started running as fast as his feet could go. He kept on running, and at one time he looked behind to check if Kitasioyia was following him. By dawn (*etamanayie esirua*) he was very far away from where he had left Kitasioyia sleeping. He had no idea of where he was heading. Then he decided to stop, climbed a tree to allow himself some rest and to figure out the location of their old *manyatta*. He had a nap on top of the tree. He used the strap of his sword to tie himself on to the tree so as not to fall.

Ole Melita set off long before dawn and started running once again in fear of Kitasioyia catching up with him. He kept on and on until sunset. By this time, he knew that he had gone very far and Kitasioyia was nowhere near him. He made up his mind that, if she came, he would spear her to death then cut her into pieces with his sword. This time, he would not be as kind as he had been.

Meanwhile, Kitasioyia was still fast asleep. Later, after the fire had gone out, in the early hours of the morning in Kimaasai *etamanayie esirua* – Kitasioyia was awakened by the craving hyenas who were feeding on the meat left by Ole Melita. The hyenas were attracted by *esong' ouna* the smell of the roasted meat and that of the leftovers of the night before. It was unfortunate for her because she wouldn't have enough time to dig her claws into the hyena's back the way she did with Ole Melita. Kitasioyia ran and jumped on top of one of the hyenas, thinking it was Ole Melita, then said, 'Oh! you thought that you had left me?' (*Aa! ijo duo iyie kitung'uayie?*)

The strange sound coming on top of his back scared the hyena to death. On hearing this, the hyena ran as fast as he could through the thick forest, Kitasioyia screaming and crying loudly from pain and banging on trees and thorns that had pierced her body. She started to plead with the hyena, 'Oh! Mr Hyena, please stop. Let me come down! Let me come off your back. I shall not repeat it again. Please stop, stop,' begged Kitasioyia to the hyena. But he ran all the more recklessly to shake off what was on his back in the depths of the thick forest, aiming to destroy Kitasioyia. He kept running on and on until Kitasioyia died!

As for Ole Melita, he continued his journey the following day, arriving in the late evening at his village. His relatives were very happy now to know that he was back at last, unharmed. He then related to them about his ordeal and the nightmares of the past few days with Kitasioyia.

The End – *Ne-iting' eba neija*

This story was told to the children to emphasize caution in what they do, and the same applies to us grown-ups. Had Ole Melita been cautious about what his friend told him, he would have not faced the above difficulties as he did. As for Kitasioyia she paid for her diabolic acts of cruelty towards Ole Melita, who had been kind to her. She died a horrible death.

There is a proverb/wise saying in Kiswahili – *Asiye funzwa na mamake, ufunzwa na ulimwengu* – literal translation: One who is not taught by his/her parents will be taught by the world, meaning a child's good character and behaviour is an outcome of his parental teaching and guidance during his youth ... If a child refuses this training it implies that he will definitely suffer when he grows up and enters into the real world – which is unfeeling and uncaring and he will learn the hard way.

A STORY OF A WOMAN WHO WAS DIVORCED FOR NOT HAVING CHILDREN

Once upon a time there was this woman who stayed for many years without having children. She had been to practically all medicine men in order to conceive but with no success. She was very sad and decided to move from her village to live in the forest to avoid meeting people who would ask her what she would do next.

One day, she met a man during her stay in the forest. They made friends after discussing about her sad life of being barren. The man promised to try to give her his time, or rather he would try to keep her company. They spent a few times together and a miracle happened. She became pregnant! She couldn't believe it but there it was! On realizing this, she moved away from the place where she was living in fear that the man might decide to take away the child on delivery. She moved to an unknown area to avoid contact with him.

On the arrival of the baby, she managed to find a huge tree – *oreteti* – with many branches and she climbed up and made a large bed with dry branches. She tied them with *inkopit* then on top she put grass for a mattress and later she added *olchoni* (hide/skin) for the baby to sleep on.

She brought up the baby inside her temporary hut in the forest. Each day she sang to the baby, '*Nemoda kulo lumbwa naayie enkaipoponi ai, lemeyiolo ele sina na yie enkaipoponi ai, osina lenkiyio nabo naayie enkaipoponi esila ai ool-mara-urau naaiyie enkaipoponi.*' (Literal translation: Oh God of all creation these Lumbuas are foolish as they do not know the anguish, oh God of all creation the pains of having a lone child, oh God of all creation, thank you for giving me my little girl with jingles that make light raining sounds.

Day after day she sang the same song. When the child was two months old she decided to take it to a safe place on top of the tree she had prepared earlier.

Day after day she went there to breastfeed the baby. She always sang the same song for the baby, and after feeding it she washed the baby, then thereafter she returned it to the bed on top of the tree.

When *enkaipoponi* started to speak she also replied when the mother sang the song every lunchtime and evening whenever she went to feed her. One day, somebody overheard her singing to the child, and this was the father of the child. The man recognized her voice and so he hid himself in a nearby bush to try to memorize the words. The whole day he stayed within that area. At lunchtime, she started singing to the child before climbing the tree. The man did not follow her at this stage because she could have seen him approaching. He waited till she was out of sight before he moved. He then followed her to a nearby bush and waited.

So far it had been all right as she had enough food for the baby. She went into her hut satisfied that her child was well and growing without much difficulties. The man followed her till she entered her hut. Day after day the woman did the same thing, going to the tree to feed her child after singing the same song. By now the child was big and could repeat the same song after her mother.

This went on for some time. The enemy also tried to

imitate the song so that the child could answer but it never worked. The child never answered. The man became very annoyed that the child didn't answer him. He kept on trying, hoping that one day the child would answer. I am her father she must answer back he thought. One day, the mother came and sang as usual but the child did not answer immediately as usual. She hesitated as she was afraid what had happened earlier that day. She was not sure, but when her mother sang for the second time she answered. Her mother then climbed the *oreteti* tree to feed her as usual. While they were together her mother asked her why she had not answered at the first instant. She explained it was because of an earlier incident when a man tried to imitate her voice. The woman was terrified and was at a loss for words as to what would become of her loved one. By now she knew that somebody was trying to steal her only child. What was she going to do now? She was in a state of shock and could not find the answer.

Enkaipoponi asked her mother what was wrong. Her mother then warned her not to answer any stranger. She then continued to warn her that she should be careful because there were bad people.

After her return to her hut, the woman was troubled by what had transpired during that day. She tried to find a solution as to how she would protect her child.

Two days later nothing happened. The man did not go back there as he was yet to master the song and try to imitate the woman properly. After the fourth day, he went back and this time he was sure it would be answered. He was right. As soon as he sang, the little girl answered. He then climbed the tree and brought her down with him. After that he chopped off her hand and left it just next to the tree, making sure that the mother would see it upon her return. He then walked a little further and then cut off her leg and put it on the footpath where the mother would pass. By this time, the child was bleeding profusely and had fainted due to loss of blood. As if that was not enough, he continued with his cruel acts, leaving the head last, close to the woman's hut.

That evening she was going as usual to feed the child,

unaware of what had happened. No sooner had she opened the door than she saw the head of the poor child cut into pieces. She started screaming and crying. She then picked the head, then the leg, then the hands, until at last she had all the pieces and she went to bury them. A few days later she hanged herself as she had nothing to live for now.

The End – *Ne-iting' eba neija*

The purpose of this story was to emphasize understanding. What the man could have done was to talk to the woman and come to a compromise about the child. The child belonged to both of them. They should have tried to find a solution in order to bring up the innocent child in more secure surroundings instead of acting that way. In life one should not make decisions while in a temper. As a result the man lost two people.

During other leisure times, Naini and other children of the village played hide-and-seek games, made dolls from the fruits of the sausage trees, *ol-darpoi* and moulded clay dolls, *in-kera e-sarng'ab.*

As a child, she also collected fresh cow dung, which was later used for repairing the huts during the rainy season or whenever there were any cracks visible on the walls caused by the hot sun. The plastering was not done by young children but rather by young ladies and older girls.

And for clothes, Naini wore *ilkarash*, two pieces of material which were usually painted brown by use of ochre (*ereko*), one knotted at the shoulder and the other around her waist. Unlike now, when ladies and young children are dressed in *lessos*, a type of sarong worn by both men and women.

Living in Europe has made her change and adjust to other ways of dressing and use of other type or ornaments to suit the climatical conditions and other cultures. As they say, when in Rome, do as the Romans do, and Naini is no exception. However, she believes it is important to preserve the African heritage and culture.

Naini used to bow her head to greet the elders as a child.

This custom, *a-ng'asaki*, which is still normal, obliges the youth to bow his/her head to an elderly person, who will then place his/her hand on the child's head. The words used will then depend on the subject – for the boy, we say *supa* to which he answers '*Epa*', for a girl we say '*takwenya*'; the latter will answer '*iko*'. Normally in Kimaasai greetings, one must wait for the other person to answer your call before proceeding with the actual salutation.

Like all Maasai children, as a child Naini grazed the calves round the kraal.

Naini had her teeth extracted while she was still living at her grandmother's home. Teeth were extracted using an extracting instrument designed for this purpose. Her first two teeth were removed from the lower jaw at the age of five years. The second set of teeth also from the lower jaw were removed a year later. When a child started losing her milk teeth she was told to throw them in the early morning towards sunrise while reciting these words '*Kolong iwa kulo ala lainei ngiroin pee kincho ilala oibor*' (direct translation 'Sun take away my brown teeth and give me white ones'). After removing these teeth, they were tied with a leather string around her neck with *Embornoti*. This teeth-removing ceremony was called *abo*. The teeth were removed to create a gap for emergency purposes, such as in times of illness when a person cannot eat, for example lockjaw, whereby an individual faints and clenches his teeth. In those days this gap enabled the family concerned to feed the invalid by passing liquids through it by means of a wooden straw called *enkiseket*. The only foods administered this way were in liquid form such as soup from boiled bones, mixed with special juices from roots or bark. This special soup was very fortifying and nutritious to drink during and after recovery from an illness. Some of these herbs are still used by the Maasai people, and some other tribes have also followed suit. In fact some of these herbs can be bought from butcheries mostly in the Maasai countryside. What Naini cannot distinguish is if these roots and stripped barks are the same ones used by her grandmother.

Naini's ears were then pierced using *ol-tidu,* a needle which was put into the fire and when it became red hot, it was then pierced through the tip of the upper part of her two lobes (*in-kitipeta*) starting with the right-hand side. A small stick was put in to prevent it from closing up, which was changed every three to four days so as to enlarge the hole. When the ears healed, the sticks were replaced with Maasai local earrings (*i-muna*).

Naini still puts on her Maasai earrings occasionally, and the lower and upper garments worn by Maasai women, together with her beadwork. As Naini looks back now, she is glad that her lower ear lobes (*i-segeruani*) were not pierced and the ear lobes extended.

The lower part of the ears are usually cut using a special knife in a circle placing a piece of wood or dried cowhide at the back of the ear lobe during the operation. Later the hole is fitted with *in-kulalen,* which are plugs, usually made of wood, inserted on the lobes of both ears soon after the operation. The operation is usually more complicated than that of *in-kitepeta* but carried out exactly the same way. Changing the plugs on both ear lobes every two or three days serves as a dressing to help the ears to heal quickly while at the same time enlarges the hole to a much bigger extent.

Her sister's ear lobes were pierced after she ran away to a neighbouring village and claimed that their grandfather had sent her for the ceremony because he was too old and his hands were no longer steady, so he could not perform the operation, but of course she lied!

Their mother had objected to the piercing as she had intended to send her to school one day. This kind of operation makes one look very different, especially if one had to put on the European's costumes instead of the usual Maasai attire and leave the holes empty without inserting *in-konito o in-kiyiaa* ornaments (ear flaps). Her sister, because her ear lobes were pierced when they were children, wears the earflaps/earrings occasionally, unlike Naini. The same applies for men, but instead of putting *in-konito o in-kiyiaa,* they put instead *i-lmintoni* usually made out of brass by the blacksmith.

When Naini was still in her grandmother's home, in her primary school, she had put on her thighs some tribal marks, known as *ilkiperat* in Kimaasai, in the company of other children of the same village just to prove that one was courageous. These marks are put on the thigh using a burning stick cut out evenly on both sides in the shape of a cigarette and then placed on the flat side of the thigh, after wetting the skin with saliva. It was then left burning until it was completely ashes. Later, the thighs were full of wounds from the burns and one was not supposed to show any kind of fear during the exercise. This operation is almost like when the incisor teeth are extracted; one must show a lot of courage and perseverance. The brand designs/marks are made by the majority of Maasai youths. The thigh brand is mainly for girls. All these decorations were supposed to add to the girl's beauty.

There was yet another brand design made by Naini's sister which is a brand on the girl's face by using the *ol-ngeriantus* plant, which is a small delicate lily flower which grows during the rains. The *ol-ngeriantus* plant has beans and sap which is rubbed into small cuttings under the skin of the face or the breast and leaves dark blue marks which is some sort of tattoo (*a-iger enkomom/il'ngeriantusi*). The marks around her breast were put by use of a needle and a razor blade. To some, these brands can cause a lot of suffering – to those with sensitive skins.

Most of the children – boys and girls – will ignite a fire by rubbing two sticks together while herding cattle. During Naini's childhood, most families object to this practice because some children at times fall sick, depending on the sensitivity and their skin reaction. Naini herself developed some problems as the self-inflicted marks became big wounds and swollen glands, and she was nearly unable to walk. She tried to hide them from being seen by her family members, otherwise she would be caned. She tried covering them with her lower garment, which made it even worse as the cloth would stick on the sores and when she tried to remove it later, it peeled off the skin, leaving it bleeding once again! This was very painful. It took several days before it was completely cured. The marks left permanent scars on her thighs, as it was meant to. Her grandmother treated her by applying some leaves on the marks after chewing them.

Naini saw her sister Nareyio putting *onl-geriantus* on her face but this time she was not tempted as she was afraid that it might bring her the same kind of complications as that of *ilkiperat*.

Listed below are some Maasai beads/ornaments worn by both men and ladies, particularly on special occasions such as circumcision, a ceremony from time immemorial which is still practised.

BEADS – MAASAI ORNAMENTS

Saen is the common name for all beads, which are either stringed together or sewn onto other material, cloth or leather. These beads have different sizes and colours. The most common being red, white, green, orange and black. They are often arranged into definite and common patterns. These are also divided into those mainly worn by women and those worn by both sexes.

ORNAMENTS FOR MARRIED WOMEN

a) *Enkitati e nkoshoke.* Made of treated hide-strap and decorated with cowrie shells (*isikira*) and used only by women to hold back the stomach after childbirth

b) *En-konito oo nkiyiaa.* These are ear ornaments worn by married women in the lower ear rim, the string hanging from one ear to the other. Also attached is *emonyorit* the marriage chain.

40

ORNAMENTS WORN BY BOTH GIRLS AND WOMEN

a) *Enkimeita*: Broad headed belt worn by girl.

b) *Enkitati nailang'a*: Beaded waist belt worn by girls

c) *Enkitati*: Loin belt worn by both women and girls to hold up *olekesena* (loin dress) – the women's one is without beads, unlike the one for girls

d) *I-mankeek*: Beaded ornaments worn by both women and girls around their necks

e) *Enkarewa*: The traditional long strings of beads suspending from *e-mankeki*

BEADS WORN BY BOTH MEN AND WOMEN

a) *Entore*: Beaded belt worn by young men around the waist

b) *Enkeene e maragit*: Strings of beads worn by *ilmuran* – warriors – on the chest and crosswise at the front as well as at the back

c) *Il-miintoni*: Small earring beads worn by old men in the hole of the lower ear rim

d) *Il-kulankoli*: A large egg-shaped bead affixed to *ol-mini-toi*

e) *Emurt narok*: Stringed beads worn by fathers around the neck as an indication of initiation of a son recovering from circumcision

f) *Ol-kataar*: Beaded strap worn by both men and women around the upper arm

g) *Imuna*: Beaded earrings worn by both men and women in the small hole in the upper ear rim. Note: for ladies, they are larger than those for men

Naini's stepfather was born of a Maasai family but unfortunately his father had passed away when he was still young.

41

He was the second-born child in a family of eleven children, amongst whom, four were twins; four had died at an early age, leaving seven children. During the colonial days, he was amongst the very few lucky Maasai to have gone to school.

After the death of their father, their mother brought them up on her own. The family cattle were taken by other relatives as she had no one to defend her. In fact this was one of the things that made her two sons get the chance to go to school. When the white people came to the Maasai homes to choose children to be taken to school, she had agreed easily. The children who had both parents were restricted and only a few agreed to let them attend school.

Naini's stepfather did not really care much about her, due to the fact that she was born elsewhere and furthermore she was not his real child. The other influencing factor was because by that time most men of his age-group – *olporror*, men who are circumcised together – had no children. The fact that he was way ahead of the others made him feel a little uncomfortable. We shall discuss about the age group later on.

By that time, Naini was between the age of six and seven years and had not started going to school. She continued with the home chores like all the other Maasai children in the village, mainly drawing water from a nearby river and herding calves around the home.

3

STARTING SCHOOL

When the time came for Naini to go to school, she was moved to go and live at Naisula's home which was closer to the school compared to her uncle's home. At Naisula's home, life became even more difficult than what she had passed through before. By then Naini had already lived in two other homes, including her grandmother's home (mother's side). While living with Naisula, Naini was one time denied by Naisula the cow that was donated to her custody by her uncle while she was staying with them. The understanding was that Naisula would keep the cow in order to milk it for Naini, but the woman never honoured that agreement. Instead she kept all the milk herself. One day she became so bad that she even refused to give Naini her midday meal and in the evening, she gave a very small share.

Naisula's daughter was always very kind to her. When she saw what her mother had done, and knowing her mother's cruelty, she gave Naini some of her own food after making sure that her mother did not see it. On another night, she did the same thing, and this time, Naini was forced by hunger to eat dry *ugali* (maize porridge) with salt as she was so hungry that she could not sleep at night.

All these things she endured bitterly. Naini looks back now and says it does not pay to take revenge or to be unkind to other people. If you wrong somebody, who knows where you will meet in the future. In conclusion, Naini says all these things have shaped her and made her aware of many things, most of all to take life seriously and try to plan.

She lived in Naisula's home until she attained ten years. After that, she was sent to a boarding school.

On one Monday morning of January 1955, Naini was woken very early to prepare herself for going to school. Being her first day, this was possible through the help of her aunty, Lemiso's wife, as she was unable to dress on her own, due to the new type of dresses which were so different from the usual Maasai attire. Although she had been wearing a dress to go to church, this did not include knickers, which she was told to wear that morning. As she tried to put on her knickers, she put both legs through one hole, unaware that each leg had its own hole. Since they were not made to measure, her two tiny thighs went through without much difficulty. But then, as she tried to stand up to walk, it fell to her knees then to the ground.

On realizing the mistake she had made, she turned them round and at last managed to wear them correctly, although she was not able to tie the straps properly because the front was facing the back. It was then that her aunt came to her rescue. Although she had seen men wearing trousers, in church, she had never really observed them closely. Back home in the village, most men and women dressed in the Maasai attire – ladies in *lesos*, young men dressed in one *leso* and old men dressed in *lesos* with, on top, either a *blacket*, leather traditional attire, or a big overcoat.

The first day Naini went to school, she was taken by her uncle Lemiso. The rest of the pupils were already on the parade. They were then directed to go to the headmaster's office to pay the school fees. While they were still at the headmaster's office the class teacher came in. Naini was then introduced to her, and taken to the classroom and introduced to the other pupils in the class.

In the classroom, she was then led to her desk. Soon after, she started shedding tears because everyone was looking at her. She got so afraid that she couldn't even look up or concentrate.

After a while she heard the bell ringing and the teacher left and another one came in and started a different lesson.

Everyone wants new encounters and new environments to be able to go forward in life, make friends and even advance socially. But Naini's first day at school was not as she expected. Having become used to home, she expected the school to provide the same hospitality. However, she was excited to have started schooling, and knowing that she would some day be able to read and write like her uncle Lemiso made her happy.

The first sight of school, the many pupils and teachers, scared her a bit. She had never seen such a big crowd all dressed in the same kind of clothing, except a few students in the church. So, this was going to be her new environment for the coming four years of primary education. Since her uncle was working by then at the African court as an interpreter, she was encouraged to think that one day she would be able to work like him. Having met other girls and boys, she was relieved to learn that she was not growing up alone; she would adapt as the others had done. She would become the most elite person in her community and feel at home among her classmates.

Naini really expected to be treated as she was at home. That was why at around ten o'clock she went to another student who seemed to be well informed (later she learnt that he was the class monitor) and asked him for gruel (*oloshoro*) not realizing in her ignorance, as Daniel explained, that here everybody needed to bring his/her food because the school did not provide any.

Daniel had to go to relieve himself, and during his few minutes of absence, he temporarily appointed Leperes to take his position. All of a sudden a sign of relief showed on Naini's face. Their first male teacher, Mr Koros, came in and introduced himself. After that, he asked who was the class monitor, and Leperes raised his hand. Daniel had not yet returned. To Naini's surprise and disappointment he summoned Leperes to go in front of the class. Then he told him bend down for a stroke of the cane, the reason being that when he entered the classroom, the pupils were making a noise. Thereafter he outlined the monitor's duties unaware

45

that Leperes was just sitting in for Daniel. He then warned them all that anybody found making a noise in the class would face the same punishment. By then Naini was trembling with fear. She started to plan to run away from school. She thought if this was how they were treated, she would not stay. Just then she heard a knock on the door and another teacher, Ole Kilgoris came in. Naini learnt his name from Daniel. Daniel, who was talking to another student, excused himself and came straight to sit down next to Naini.

Having been prepared for formal education, they did not in fact learn much on the first day. This was because every pupil was expected to go through an orientation period of one day before going into class work. When her uncle had brought her to school that morning, he had advised her to be observant and follow all the details the teacher would put across. Bearing this in mind, she did her best.

When she joined standard one, she did not know what to expect. Initially, the lessons seemed very, very difficult, but gradually she got used to writing on her small black board, using a piece of white chalk.

Two hours or so later, Naini needed to go to the toilet, but she felt too shy to walk up to the teacher to request permission as she would not find the right words. She just could not face him on this issue! Her mind reflected back home. At her uncle's home, whenever she felt like it, she would just go into the bush without alerting anybody, so she did not see why she should tell the teacher. It did not make sense. So you can imagine what happened. She just stood up and headed straight to the toilet! Inside the toilet, she struggled to untie her knickers for the first time – the urge was so pressing that she nearly let loose. But to avoid this, she pressed the knickers to one side and then urinated. On her return to the classroom, their teacher realized that Naini was too shy, and came up with an idea after this incident. He would send her to the toilet without asking permission.

By the end of the day and after this practice, Naini gathered courage, although it took her a few days to acquire friends. Once or twice she had missed her lessons and went home, only to find her uncle, who encouraged Naini gently to go back to school and continue with her lessons. To encourage Naini, he said, 'One without education has no future.' For the rest of her schooling years, she always heard those words ringing the bell at the back of her mind.

Her friend Lemayian, who had lice on his head during the parade, had his hair cut by Ole Koros. The teacher walked into the staffroom and soon returned with a large pair of scissors and began carving lines on Lemayian's hair. He made one large line from his forehead, making him look as if he was bald-headed. And on a second thought, he once again took the scissors through to the back of his neck. He then criss-crossed the head to the bottom of both ears, making sure that he deliberately left some parts untouched which looked like small mountains.

Lemayian told them the following day that, on arriving home his mother promised to shave off the remaining hair first thing in the morning because one cannot be shaved at sunset. At sunrise, his mother shaved him. But first of all she wet the hair with water and soap. As was customary, she started from the right-hand side, using a sharp knife (*ol-murunya*) and shaved the whole head clean. After that Lemayian's new clean-shaven head looked like horns would grow in the next few days.

Lemayian was not the only one to be shaved. Naini also had her head shaved several times in her youth, even before she started going to school, and naturally during the ceremonial occasions.

Having *i-lashe* on the clothes or on the children's heads was very common. Naini once asked a friend to help her to hunt and destroy the *i-lashe* on her great-great-grandparent's. lower garment, which was made of pure sheep leather (*o-leke-sena*). First, they spread the garment in the sun, the inside facing the sun, so as to go through each binding. No sooner had they done this, than *i-lashe* came out from hiding in numbers to try to escape from the hot sun. This was the time to act not to let any escape. With their fingernails, they crushed them to death. From some, those who had had their fill, the blood would spill after the explosion of their thin skins, while some were just dry.

As for her great-great-grandmother, who had lost her sight, she requested Naini to put the *i-lashe* on the palm of her hand and in turn, by the feel of her right-hand thumb and index-finger, she caught them and put them straight into her mouth to bite them in revenge. After this, she then spat the blood and the tiny parasites out. Then she told Naini and her friend that she had made sure that the little parasites would never drain anyone else's blood in the future.

For curiosity's sake, Naini put one in her mouth and bit it to find out how her great-great-grandmother felt. It was so horrible that she nearly threw up. In the meantime her friend almost died with laughter; she laughed until her ribs were aching and tears rolling down her cheeks. Naini joined in the laughter. After all this, her great-great-grandmother too was curious to find out what had happened and why they were so happy.

Naini told her what she had done. She also laughed, then asked did you think it was sweet?'

'I thought so, and I was curious to find out,' Naini said, 'but I now know that it is not. In fact I don't know how you manage to do that every time! and how can you tolerate such an unpleasant taste!'

After that Naini gave her back her *o-lekesena*. She in turn girdled it around her waist using *en-kitati*. Then she lay down on the green grass and asked Naini to climb on her back to give her a massage using her tiny feet, with the support of her walking stick Naini stood upright to do it. After that she handed back her walking stick then they all moved to sit under the shade. Naini requested her to tell them a story, but she refused, saying '*meinosi enkatini dama*', meaning stories are not told during the day.

That evening, she slept very peacefully after the events of the day.

48

4

EDUCATION

Naini first went to school at the age of seven. It was her uncle's persuasion which at last convinced her stepfather Olomunyak to send her there. She underwent her primary education at Narok, which was five miles from where they lived. Due to lack of transport in the area Naini had to walk the long distance of ten miles in bare feet even in the rain and the cold. It was not easy for her considering that she was still very young. But this did not discourage her from pursuing her education, because of her determination. And because she was not the only one going to school from that neighbourhood, she did not see why she should not make it if the rest of the folks from the area could! With this in mind, it gave her the drive.

Naini's school timetable flowed from Monday to Friday, 8.00 a.m. to 4.00 p.m. daily, for nine months a year – January to March, then Easter holidays, May to the August holidays, and then September to December for the Christmas holidays.

Recess time was at 10.30 a.m. and after that they had PE. This exercise included cross-country, long jump and netball. Naini was also an active choir member and took part in most of the school plays.

It was during the month of January when the school had just reopened for the first term of her second consecutive year that Naini experienced some hardships because of the weather. It was late one afternoon when the rain started and continued to stream down. The darkness closed in even

49

further, giving a portentous feel of a dark night. Naini had to return home that evening from school in the heavy rain. Everywhere grew darker due to the thick clouds, except for the light from the lightning. Large cold drops of rain soaked her from head to toe as she had no umbrella or raincoat. She would run a short distance then go under the trees for shelter from the heavily pouring rain. Water dripped on her school books and she got angry at the rain, wishing she didn't have to walk the long distance. But she knew that she had no choice except to keep running to keep warm. As it was a Friday, she was relieved by the thought of the coming weekend. At least she could stay home for two days!

On arriving home, she removed her school uniform then rinsed it and removed the water to make it dry (*amoniraa enkare pee etoyu.*) She then put on her two *shukas*, the Maasai day-to-day attire, though she was feeling cold to the extent that her teeth could be heard chattering. She sat by the fire to warm herself and to dry her school books, which were totally soaked. Carefully she dried them leaf by leaf, paying special attention that they did not get torn. Although she paid so much attention to drying her books, on some of the pages the ink was washed away and she could hardly read what she had written. This took longer than she had anticipated and she had other things to do before the end of the evening. The rain had come unexpectedly that day. Earlier that morning, there had been no sign of rain, the sky was clear blue with no clouds.

Later that evening, she did her homework as usual before the evening meal. After dinner she was so tired that after that she went straight to bed, which was unusual for her. On other days, Naini usually helped in the domestic chores, such as hewing wood, plastering the house when necessary, drawing water, milking the cows and bringing in the young calves into the calves' pen (*olale loo lasho*).

Inkimaliani are constructions made from twigs, grass and bound together with strips of bark from trees (*inkopit*) and cemented with cow dung (*emodioi oo nkishu*), and generally constructed after the kraal has been built. The majority of

50

the inhabitants during Naini's youth lived in this type of home. There are no nails involved in these huts, which were mainly built inside the settlement (*enkang*), which was a homestead usually occupied by several elders with their families.

Now, this type of habitation is disappearing, due to the land demarcation which is taking place in many districts in Kenya including Maasailand.

The cattle enclosure is usually cleaned by the women of the village. They put away the fresh cow dung and at times *o-lo-kidong'oi* (mud formed from rain and old cow dung) and put it at the dunghill (*ol-chala*) inside the settlement and especially that which is removed from the calves' pen (*olale*). Each evening, as soon as the sun went down, the main village *en-kishomi* was shut up after the return of cows from their grazing.

Each evening, Naini did her homework with light from a lantern lamp, or sometimes she put a hole in a tin lid and inside put some paraffin on a piece of old material and lit a wick to burn oil and produce light. This is known as *karuboi* in Kiswahili. The hurricane lamp, an oil lamp or candlestick with a tall glass chimney to keep the flames from being blown out was much better than the *karuboi* as it produces less smoke, but in those days, not many people had them in Naini's village. While using *karuboi*, sometimes the room would get very smoky due to the firewood, and it smelt bad because the lamp also produced a lot of smoke. Nevertheless, Naini preferred to have it burning than do her homework in the darkness or using only the firelight. At times there was no money to buy the paraffin for the tin lamp. This meant she had to make do without either lamp. At such times, she was forced to use firelight to enable her to see what she had to write, or try to do it before darkness. It was difficult but she was determined, otherwise she would be caned by the class teacher for failing to do her homework.

In those days there was no electricity in the area, even though she thinks this could not have helped her situation considering that it was difficult even to afford some paraffin for her. She was, however, very grateful for what her uncle's family had done for her, knowing that it was not their responsibility to cater for her, but her uncle Lemiso took that trouble. He was very kind to her, offering what was available within his means.

For cooking, the majority of the people in those days used firewood. The fire place was a hole dug in the ground inside the hut with three stones (*isoito lenkima*) placed to support the pots.

In the Maasai tradition, there was always an *oleng'oti* in the fire. This was a log of wood that was kept alight for days. A few people during those days used paraffin stoves for cooking.

At the weekend, Naini washed her school uniform, which comprised of two khaki dresses, two pairs of cotton knickers which were tied on the left side with a string, and two sweaters. She also had a school bag made of cloth for carrying her books, but she had no shoes.

For washing her clothes, she used bar soap, and as she had no pail or basin, she washed them on top of a big stone in a shallow area at the river bank. She would then lay them on the high grass to dry in the sun and later iron them using an old charcoal iron box filled with red-hot charcoal.

To crown it all, she had a bath, then she put on her day-to-day Maasai *ilkarash*.

In her childhood, Naini wore the traditional attire every weekend, like all the other children, except on Sundays when going to church. On this day, she always wore her rubber shoes and a special dress used only for going to church. On return from church she would remove it and keep it until the following Sunday.

Naini went to a church near her former school where she joined the Sunday school class and was later baptized. She also joined the church choir and proceeded to her first holy communion. During Christmas in those days, people went from one home to another singing Christmas carols and just before midnight, Naini and the rest would go to church. She has pleasant memories of such gatherings.

After her bath, Naini returned to the river, which was a

mile away, to fetch water, using a clay pot which she carried on her head. The pot was carried in a special way with *enkatiet* a round bracelet pad of grass used to steady pots and gourds, placed between her head and the pot. The *enkatiet* was made out of green grass (*emurrua*) and bark string (*enkopito*). All the Maasai ladies, including young girls carried water with it. Its main functions were for balance and to minimize discomfort on the women's heads, which were traditionally always clean-shaven. The *enkatiet* was also used during special occasions when native beer was being served and also while it was being fermented (*emuka inaishi*). It was also placed beneath the earthen pot in the *oltiren*, the bedroom of a Maasai house which also serves as a fire-place/brewing area when it was being drunk.

The weekend afternoons were the time to gather firewood. With a panga, Naini cut the dried branches and carried them on her back, tied together with *enkeene*, leather straps made from cow hides. The leather ropes were made by cutting narrow strips from fresh cow's hide, drying them and then weaving them into long lengths.

To put the firewood on her back, Naini had to sit down beside the tied bunch, secure the leather straps on each shoulder, side by side, then ask someone to lift it up from the back while she was still sitting down. To stand, she bent forward on her knees then got up on her feet. When offloading, she would again sit down then remove the straps from her shoulders. When there was no one to help her lift the load from behind, she arranged the firewood on a slope, making it easier to tilt it onto her back.

There were other duties to be done, such as milking, looking after sheep and calves, cleaning the animal shed and collecting cow dung from the *boma* and heaping it at one place for later use, in case it rained, for plastering the hut's roof (*a-murishore*). The collected cow dung was smeared on top of the thatched mud hut so as to prevent leaks during the rainy season. It must be noted that customarily it was the Maasai women who built *il-muumuni*, the temporary leather-covered tent-like huts also known as *parnati*. Naini shared the duties with the other girls of her age. Young girls were slowly taught their domestic responsibilities by their mothers and older girls.

As a child, Naini also drove the cows several times to the river to drink water and other times to eat *embolio* – salt lick. When she was a little older, she also skinned *ol-ashe* (calves) in the company of older boys – calves that had died at birth. Later, they made *ol-kutu* – a dummy – from the dead calf's skin, stuffed it with dry grass and used it while milking the cow in place of the calf. The skin was first dried on a flat ground while held by *in-cheito* (wooden pegs) to prevent it from rotting. It would take several days before the cow discovered that her calf was dead.

While milking the cow, her grandmother used a different calabash for each cow. Naini enjoyed drinking milk from her *enkoti* calabash and especially when it was still warm and full of foam. At times, she even drank milk by milking it directly into her mouth (*en-dasata*). Most children did this sometimes while herding cattle.

The weather was very unpredictable at times. Some days had lots of sunshine, others were cloudy with rain or storms, with lightning splashing in series and deafening thunder. The conditions were so difficult as there were no transportation facilities available, and Naini had to go everywhere barefoot. Shoes were nearly unheard of except during Christmas time, when most families offered their children a pair of rubber shoes which was supposed to last them one year before they were given another pair. Naini used to wear her pair of shoes only on Sundays when going to church.

On Sundays when Naini used to put on shoes, she was occasionally embarrassed because the congregation of the church stared at her as if she had abnormal legs. This was true somehow because the shoes were sometimes bigger than her tiny feet and this made her walk as if she had jiggers on her toes. Most of the time the rubber shoes were one or two sizes larger than her actual size, so that she did not outgrow them quickly!

She was even more embarrassed when young children ran

around her, wanting to feel what was on her feet. This was because during her youth, most children either walked barefoot or wore open sandals made from either cowhide or from old car tyres. Naini was not the only one to wear oversized shoes as a child.

On other days, the majority wore sandals made from cowhide prepared by the natives of the village. The rubber shoes never lasted very long, due to the rain and mud. It was also difficult to keep them clean. Naini never wore proper shoes until much later and this was even after going to the Intermediate School.

At her school, they always prayed every morning before going for their classes. During her school days, there were not as many children going to school as now in her village. This is not surprising, because many people in her home area did not know the value and meaning of education. Some lived far away from the centres where the schools were situated and there were no permanent roads, and transportation facilities were also not available.

During that period, there were also those who were not ready to accept the new changes of life and who believed that those who went to school would get lost in the towns. Our nomadic way of life also played a big role, says Naini. Families moved from one area to another in search of greener pastures for their domestic animals. Unlike now – the Maasai no longer migrate as before. They have settled in the family lands, which they can now cultivate and sell their products, to facilitate payment of their children's school fees and the buying of school books and uniforms. The farm products are usually sold in the open market.

When the Maasai people met in the market place, they would exchange greetings, such as, 'How is everybody in your village?' (*Kejaa olorere teina alo inyi?*) The other answers, '*Kira supati*' – We are all right. Are the cows and the people well? (*Ai-supati nkishu ol-tung'anak?*) Yes we are all right with the cattle ('*Ee supati iyiook nkishu ol-tung'anak.*') One then goes on to narrate the events and the reasons for their coming to the market: '*Kietuo na duo sii iyiook sokoni aapuonu*

aa-mir inkishu pee kitum iropiyiani nikipuo alakie sukuul oo nkera'
(We have come to the market to sell some cattle in order to obtain some money for school fees for the children). At the end of each sentence, the teller ends by saying, '*Niako taalelo*' – and so it came about.

The things which were mostly sold and bought in the market were beads, axes, knives, spears, native gowns, tobacco, snuff, honey, milk and domestic animals such as cows, sheep and goats. At times they were exchanged in barter trade. Most of these, especially the animals, were sold to raise money for school fees or to obtain cash for buying foodstuffs and other commodities necessary for their cattle such as salt and cattle-dip or drugs. Most families had no other source of income.

When Naini went to school, the fees were five shillings, which at that time was an amount difficult to obtain. Some families did not allow their children to go to school because they were not willing to sell their cattle or any of their goats as they believed this would diminish their only wealth.

These days, whatever the financial situation, most families try to generate finances for their children's education to ensure they are not chased away from school for lack of school fees and also give priority to all the requirements of their children's education. Nearly everyone has learnt that education is important for the development of the individual concerned and for the community as a whole. For sure we have tried to send children to school, but this is not enough, Naini believes. We must try to catch up with the fast-moving world and be competitive in job-seeking development of our people in years to come.

The Maasai as a people have been good organizers since time immemorial. Taking into account that long before the European came we had rulers, chiefs and courts, there is no reason why we cannot do it now. The same organization format can be extended to see to it that our children go to school without fail, perhaps by creating an education foundation for them, whereby every working Maasai contributes a fee towards the fund. Even those who are not working can contribute by perhaps selling one goat per family per year. Those who are working overseas could also contribute towards the same goal and have receipts issued for accounting purposes. Further to this, a committee could be set up so that any family wishing to register students in a school can approach the committee for school fees. Priority should be given to the poor families and to those with many children, if possible.

We hope that with good management and dedication from good organizers we shall succeed and survive the fast impact and the many changes so as to build a better place for the young generation. Our sons should not all end up in big towns being watchmen! It is due to this that Naini is suggesting the idea of raising a special trust fund so as to eradicate illiteracy once and for all in Maasai land. It is very discouraging and painful to think that all our warriors will end up as watchmen. The only solution to eradicate this situation forever is for the Maasai people to team up together and join hands for the improvement of the welfare of the Maasai children – and send all the children to school irrespective of their sex. By so doing, we provide better opportunities for them in the future to take up development activities in our society for generations to come.

Denying them their right to take up education, we stand to blame as parents. Let us be united, request our beloved government to better us by building more institutions of higher learning and boarding schools within the Maasai land for the Maasai children, as in most cases they abandon school due to lack of accommodation, especially during the rainy seasons when the rivers flood to an unpassable extent. This is so because most of the rivers have no permanent bridges and at times the rains sweep away the wooden bridges.

Besides all these obstacles, we must wake up and react and take the education of our children seriously as this is the only solution to rule out our backwardness and this is also the strongest weapon for advancement in the society we live in today. This is Naini's word for her dear brothers and sisters of the Maa Society.

The Maasai children could positively accept school life if their parents could settle in one place instead of retaining the nomadic lifestyle. The headmasters of the schools concerned should find a way of approaching the parents in the surrounding neighbourhood with an aim of creating awareness of the problems confronting them and their children. The guidance should be extended beyond the school years through assisting the Maasai children at large especially after their exams. The '8–4–4' system introduced in 1985 provides for eight years of primary, four years of secondary and a minimum of four years of university education, with selection examinations required to pass from one stage to the next.

Some children are left out of secondary school selection because they do not know how to find other schools and neither do their uneducated parents, especially in cases where they have not been admitted to the school of their choice. And those of us who have experienced the sweetness of education and have harvested good fruits from that education should encourage the rest to follow suit.

Naini puts a lot of emphasis on education as she feels that had she had a chance to go for higher learning she would have done better than she has. This is the reason why she is advising others to continue if they get a chance to do so. Naini knows that school fees have become a great burden to parents, taking into account that the Maasai depend on sale of livestock for income. Culturally, milk is a major food among the Maasai and at the same time livestock is used as the bride price. The herds are decreasing while demands are increasing day after day due to the ever rising cost of living. This fact too is also one of the reasons why we should take education seriously. The leaders in those remote areas should assist and advise parents who cannot raise school fees for their children who qualify to join form one on how to seek assistance. Parents should not be turned down when they approach on serious matters touching society and especially those concerning education. Instead, the leaders could organize small *harambees* (support groups) to raise the required amounts to meet at least part if not the whole amount. This special attention should be accorded to children who come from poor families but manage to excel in their exams in spite of lack of modern facilities during their schooling.

Some of the male students were quite old when joining Naini's primary school. Some even had beards. Sometimes these older boys challenged teachers to fist fights. But this never happened as teachers knew how to avoid such ugly scenarios. The late enrolment was attributed to the lack of permanent residence of families. Students were forced to miss school sometimes even for two terms.

A lot of changes have taken place in Naini's homeland, such as land demarcation showing who owns what acreage with allocated title deeds. This has greatly helped the Maasai in this area, enabling the majority of them to borrow money for agricultural use which could not have been possible in the past when the land was under communal ownership due to the pastoral ways of life. Many modern constructions have been built, such as shops, hotels and permanent residential buildings, banks and post offices, all with electricity and telephone services.

One long-standing problem in Maasailand is the availability of medical services. People have to walk many miles to reach them due to lack of transportation. This situation is made worse by lack of roads to the interior of the country.

Maasai towns should be equipped with workshops not only to enable women from such areas to join together but also to enable them to earn their own upkeep and that of their offspring. It would also afford the women a sense of self-respect and purpose, and even as a project, it would give them a place to go to socialize while learning to cope with this fast-developing world.

Looking back on the girls of her *e-sirit*, Naini has a feeling that if there had been such places of re-creation, they would have not let themselves grow very old unnecessarily because of neglecting themselves. A woman can be as productive as a man even in the countryside, if given the facilities. Unity for all Kenyan, and all the people of the world!

Together we are brighter than the sun
Together we are bigger than the sea
Together we will be the best
Together we will be the greatest!

During Naini's youth, children went to school at the age of seven and then underwent four years of primary education. After that, they took Common Entrance, and thereafter they entered intermediate school. After four years again, they sat for KAPE (Kenya African Primary Education). Naini's marks were acceptably high in the aggregate.

In those days, at 15 years, children did Kenya African Secondary School Examination (KASSE).

Naini used to run all the way to school, stopping only occasionally to catch her breath, as being late meant that she would be punished. Late comers were punished so severely that some children never returned to school thereafter as they developed a hatred due to such punishment which often included bending over, holding on to the ear lobes, arms passing through the legs, and receiving strokes of the cane on the bottom.

Children were inspected every morning by the teacher between 8.00 and 8.30 a.m. to ensure that fingernails, ears and uniforms were clean. Those who were found having not had a bath or brushed their teeth or cut their finger-nails were beaten and sent off to wash themselves before returning to class. Toothbrushes then were made from branches of trees and used with a piece of charcoal, which was believed to keep teeth white. For bathing, some used soap and others used some leaves from certain trees which produced some kind of foam. The latter was more common among children from poor families who could not afford a piece of soap. Fortunately there was a river not far from the school, where the students washed. The school toilets were built of bricks and iron-sheet roofs and a pit latrine, which was covered with a wooden lid when not in use to prevent the smell from spreading and keep out flies. They were located at the back yard of the school a few yards from the classrooms. Teacher

Ole Leng'oi, as Naini's teacher was called, was totally against the general belief that those who went to teach in the big towns or to study would get lost. Having known the importance of education, he realized it was for the betterment of the individual. Ole Leng'oi was a hard-working person and a darling of the local community. He was serious, slim, tall and sportive, and of light complexion. He wore a moustache and close-trimmed beard. When he smiled his white teeth shone between his small lips. For his attire, he wore black-laced shoes, blue long socks folded under the knees. He also wore short khaki trousers which were ironed with starch with very sharp pleats, a leather belt and, to crown it, a white vest and a short-sleeved shirt. He also wore a wristwatch and his fingernails were well groomed. Teacher Ole Leng'oi set a high demonstration of neatness.

He used to send some of the older boys to his house which was within the school compound to clean it or fetch fire wood from the nearby forest or to chop or to split wood using an axe in the forest for his own personal use or even to wash dishes. These were the so-called 'normal' duties assigned to the pupils by the teachers from time to time. But these duties were disgraceful to the Maasai youth, especially those who were already circumcised, as they were regarded as women's chores.

Although he was strict, Ole Leng'oi was always willing to assist any pupil in whatever he/she had not understood in class. He treated pupils with respect. Some of them were nearly his age! He knew how to encourage them to continue with school, knowing only too well that if he was too harsh with them, they might never return back to school and that was the last thing he would have let happen. He wanted the Maasai children to go on learning.

Ole Leng'oi's greatest aim was to expose the Maasai youth to the many changes taking place and to prepare them to be self-reliant in the future in running their homes, especially if they had to work in towns. Teacher Ole Leng'oi taught for many years. He has long since retired, having seen many of his pupils, both boys and girls, go through education which was his desire! He is now an old man, but to his former pupils he is looked upon as a friend and also as a model for carrying forward education in that part of Kenya. His efforts will always serve as an example to those who passed through his hands, for the knowledge and encouragement without which many would have dropped out of school. Bravo Ole Leng'oi, we dearly appreciate your efforts.

5

SECONDARY SCHOOL

Naini finished her primary education after four years. Her uncle Lemiso had suggested that she continue to secondary level. He and her stepfather, Ol-omunyak, both agreed to share the responsibility of paying her school fees until she completed her education. She had performed well in the Common Entrance Examination, scoring good points which enabled her to be admitted into one of the secondary schools. She was then transferred to a boarding school which was very, very far from her home town where she stayed for nearly four years, going home only over the holidays every three months.

All along Lemiso remained very kind to her, further extending his willingness to have her in his home even after her primary education. She stayed at his home during the one-month holiday away from the boarding school. This she appreciated very, very much.

When Naini's school closed at the end of the year for the terminal and Christmas holidays, they were informed to report to the school the first week of January for their examination results. She was overjoyed to learn from the headmaster that her results were very good. She also learnt that she was top in her school, having attained the highest points in the whole class for that year. She was further informed that she had been offered a place in Narok Secondary school (DEB), as it was called in those days. After letting her read her results, the headmaster put it in a sealed envelope and addressed it with Lemiso's name.

After a small speech, Headmaster Ole Leng'oi congratulated Naini for her outstanding performance. He concluded by telling them that the lorry that was going to take them to school would pick them up there by 8.00 a.m., stressing that they should be punctual. On arriving home, Naini spread the good news of her progress to her relatives and friends. To her uncle Lemiso, she handed over the testimonial result slip given by the headmaster. After reading it he too congratulated her on her exemplary performance.

She was to report at the school by the end of that month with all her things so as to travel with the other students to the new school.

Naini was among the first Maasai girls to go to the secondary school, if not the only one from Uasi Nkishu in 1959, and among the first girls to go to primary school in her home area after the passing of a resolution by Maasai elders in 1954 on girls' education.

To Naini, it was like a dream. She had never boarded a car before, let alone travelled in a lorry, even though she had seen a police Land Rover once and a drawing of a car in the classroom. Their teacher had explained that a Land Rover was more powerful than a saloon car. She was really looking forward to going to her new school.

Remembering Ole Leng'oi's warning not to come late, Naini was the first to arrive at the meeting point. She had woken up very early that morning so as to arrive on time, accompanied by her relatives and friends who helped her carry her metal box. Some wept as they bid her farewell, advising her to go and work hard and to write letters to them whenever possible. She also held back tears. It was sad to leave her home town, her friends and family.

Everything went as planned. All the students were there on time. The trip was not an enjoyable one as it was long, bumpy and very, very dusty. The hot sun made it more uncomfortable and made her feel very thirsty.

It was quite an experience for Naini travelling for the first time in a vehicle. It seemed unreal that one could be carried for many miles sitting without using any energy at all. Each time the lorry negotiated a bend or a corner, she tried to control its movement by sitting upright and tried to take her weight to the opposite side! When the lorry turned left, she would force her weight to the right. When the lorry turned right, she would force her weight to the left, but to no avail. She was puzzled as it did not stop the lorry from swaying. By the time she arrived at their destination, she felt exhausted although she never mentioned this to anyone, assuming that the rest of the students felt the same way. She never got to find this out. Someday perhaps, she might get a chance to meet her former friends to share their views. They might have wanted to tell others too. They had travelled through the Loita plains past Ololulung'a through to Narok town. Despite all these hardships, she was never discouraged to discontinue with her education.

At the school, uniforms and books were provided. Boarding-school life was preferable with the assured regular meals and accommodation. In primary school, she had to carry her own food, which she used to hide inside the grass in the forest! There was never any guarantee that she would find her food on return during the lunch break. Sometimes it was half eaten by rats or she would just miss the spot where she had hidden it earlier that morning. There was no canteen within the school compound, neither was there a store or a proper place to keep food.

They had arrived very late that day at their new school. On arrival, the teachers were there to meet them and to welcome them to their 'temporary' home. That same evening, they were supplied with school uniform, metal plate, spoon, fork, knife, blanket and a mattress each. They were then assigned double-decker beds in pairs. All these items provided were marked according to the owner's registration number. On entering the school each student was given a personal number to avoid any duplication in case of loss. The items were also accounted for. If any got lost the cost for replacing the item(s) was deducted from the caution money, and once the amount was exhausted, the student concerned would have to pay more money the following term.

The morning after their arrival, they were woken up very early as the head girl had set the alarm clock for 6.00 a.m. the previous night in order to allow them ample time to do all what was to be done before 8.00 a.m. They took their showers in turn, dressed quickly in their khaki uniforms then proceeded for their breakfast after making their beds. The older girls assisted the younger ones, showing them how to make them. After that, they washed the dishes.

The first three days were spent on demonstration of one thing or the other by the older girls and clearing the grass in the school compound. Lessons started the same week. To Naini, the whole exercise was a series of new happenings, but she was quick to adjust to the new environment and way of life from that of her homestead. It was the first time in her life she had slept on a spring bed and in a permanent, stone building. And that was not all, it was also her first time she had seen a Tiley Lamp with light as bright as the sun, she thought! Her eyes were not accustomed to such bright light, as back in the countryside she used a paraffin lamp which was not as strong as this one.

Naini had mixed feelings. She missed home, her family and especially her former classmates, but at the same time she appreciated the new surroundings, especially the fact of not having to travel long distances every day in the hot sun and at times in heavy rain. It didn't take long, though, for her to adapt to the swift exposure and gradually she acquired new friends at her new school.

Every morning they went to the parade at 8.00 a.m. for cleanliness inspection and thereafter they prayed before proceeding to their respective classrooms. The school timetable was similar to that of the primary school. However, the weekend duties were different except the washing of the uniforms. The matron was very hard on them; they had to work a lot so as to win the inter-dormitories weekly competitions. The school was mixed, i.e. boys and girls together.

Students did practically all the school cleaning! This entailed duties such as mopping the floor of the dormitory, washing toilets, cleaning windows, planting and weeding the school (*shamba*) garden, watering the flowers, cutting grass around the dormitory compound and finally putting murram and compressing it down with flat wooden bars. Water was also sprinkled on the dusty road to reduce the dust. The dormitory floor was scrubbed using soap and water several times then later dried using a rag or mop till it was shining, and Naini could see her own reflection in the floor. So was the toilet and the shower room although they were built apart from the dormitory. During the night if one wanted to urinate, a large tin was provided, which was emptied in the toilet each morning by the older girls.

For Naini, life was not a smooth road. Unlike some other students, her parents were not in a position to buy her some necessary commodities such as sugar or even cream for applying to her body. Most of the time she had to rely on friends or even beg. Sometimes it was so bad that after eating her meals, she would apply the oil left on her plate to soothe her dry skin. Having no alternative, this was better than nothing, since it helped prevent her skin from cracking. At her home village body oil never lacked as they used sheep oil on the skin.

The term was almost ending, and by now every student was eagerly looking forward to the closing day to return to their villages. The students would break for a one-month holiday. They all prepared their school uniforms and packed them into the metal boxes (*osanduku le mabati*) ready to depart to their respective homes. There was transport, and after everybody boarded, it departed to different parts of Maasailand.

Once in the lorry, Naini watched civilization fade away the moment the lorry that carried them turned onto the dusty road that led to their home area, leaving the tarmac road from Narok town behind after the Uaso Nyiro bridge. The dust stirred by the lorry's movement as it passed through the Loita plains formed a huge cloud behind them. It resembled the dustclouds stirred by the fast-moving Safari Rally cars. Nearly every part of their bodies and the clothes they were wearing were as red as ochre! It was hard to distinguish the clothes they were wearing from the body of the lorry, which was also covered by the dust. One could have thought that all had grey hair from the look of it due to the brown soil. Today Naini equates their eyelids to those of a model who had applied heavy make-up. The hot sun and thirst made her lips crack and every part of her body felt sticky because of the dust and sweat dripping from her body from the heat. And so it was, each time the school closed and when it reopened.

The lorry travelled all the way with the roof open, except once when it started raining and the driver stopped to fit in the canvas to prevent the rain falling on them. All along the plains she saw a lot of wildlife which she admired very much: the antelopes, wildebeests and zebras, and not forgetting the elephants who sometimes blocked the untarmacked road by felling trees.

After a short drive, they saw some buffaloes grazing at a distance. This reminded Naini of a story she was told by her uncle about a running competition between a buffalo and a chameleon. The buffalo had always undermined the chameleon, claiming that she was too small and weak, that the only thing she could do was to change colour. The chameleon became annoyed so that she told the buffalo that, despite his might, she could run as fast as he and she was more intelligent than him.

They agreed to compete early the following day. The elephant was their referee. The chameleon requested that the buffalo be under the tree, she on top of the tree. When the elephant roared and lifted his trunk, the buffalo started running as fast as his feet could carry him. On arriving at the finishing point, another elephant was there to witness that competition. To his surprise, the two arrived at the same time! The buffalo nearly stepped on the chameleon when suddenly she cried. 'Please watch your foot, don't step on me.' He was so shocked to learn that the chameleon arrived the same time as he. The elephant too was impressed by the outcome of the competition. When interviewed by the elephant on how she managed to do that, she said, 'It is not the size of the body that matters but the intelligence. Since I can change colours, while you and the buffalo thought I was on top of the tree, I jumped and clicked to the buffalo's tail. As a matter of fact he carried me all through that distance!' The two respected the chameleon afterwards.

In true life, it implies that one should not underestimate anyone.

Deep in her thoughts, Naini hoped she would one day get a chance to work in the travel industry after her education so that she could visit the national parks and see the natural plains. After a while she dozed off. On the way to their destination, they stopped to relieve themselves, hiding behind the small bushes and at certain areas behind high grass.

The trip usually took a whole day, and they arrived at their destination at sunset. On arrival at the central place, which was Naini's former primary school, everyone was told to alight and reminded not to leave any of their belongings. Her mind reflected on the old days when she had to walk five miles home. She was now faced by the same distance and had to trek it once again after the three months of rest. She carried her box on her head but its heavy weight slowed her down so that she could not reach her home before dark. That night, she was forced to put up at a relative's home. The following morning, she woke up very early and started walking before the sun rose too high, to avoid its strong heat. She at last arrived at her village as they finished milking the cows.

On arrival, she was given a rousing welcome with hugs and kisses from her relatives, who were pleased to have her at home once again. To older men and women she respectfully bowed her head to greet them. She shook hands with her friends, and the younger children in turn too bowed their heads for her to lay her hand on in greeting, saying '*supa*' to the boys and '*takwenya*' to the girls. While having breakfast together, they exchanged news on past and current happenings. Naini spent her first school holidays happily with her uncle's family and former classmates who came to visit her from time to time.

A few days after her arrival, she was treated at the local dispensary for the eye infection trachoma (*enkeeya oo nkonyek*) caused by the dust. This problem she experienced each time she travelled. The mud huts with straw roofs and wooden shutters (*orike*) became very smoky, sometimes causing more irritation to the already infected eyes. One time Naini had to put her whole face through the hole for some hours (*elusie/enkutukutet*) in order to get some breeze to relieve her painful eyes, because the hut had no windows. This was not surprising. The *elusie* is a small hole in the wall that serves as a window to bring in fresh air and is also used for peeping outside. The *elusie* is also used to bring in some light during the day and by night it is shut by use of an old rug or cloth (*e-nkarasha musana naikenieki elusie/e-nkutukutet*).

Skin disease such as scabies (*il-pepedo*) were also unbearably common because of the communal accommodation. But these were just minor skin disorders which were easily treated. Naini was treated twice or so because of *il-pepedo*. During that period, to be able to relieve herself from the intense itching, she used a dry maize cob. This offered a pleasing change, without using her fingernails, which would leave scars. Thereafter, she washed the area infected with salty water. Here are some Maasai sayings and riddles which Naini learnt in the late night round the fire.

MAASAI SAYINGS:

1   *Epuonu ilimot anaa in-kilong'i* – Events follow each other like days.

2   *E-kueniyie ol-chata oika olotii en-kima ne meyiolo ajo ninye e-itokini ainok!* – The piece of wood which is in the kiln laughs at the one which is in the fire not realizing that the same fate will befall it.

3   *E-iloikino i-motioo en-kima* – Pots take turns or are put in the fire in turns.

(The last two sayings imply that you might laugh at somebody who is in a difficult situation without realizing that the same thing could happen to you, like killing somebody for money and overlooking the fact that someone else could also be paid to kill you. One should try to do more good than evil towards the human race.

70

4 *Meitong'ojin ol-kikuei lo-likai tung'ani likai tung'ani* – A thorn in somebody else's foot cannot make another limp.

5 *Memurut emurt en-dukuya* – The neck cannot bypass the head (meaning that a child cannot bypass his father's decision).

6 *Meram oleleo le moti ole nkukuri* – A piece from a broken clay pot cannot mend a broken calabash (It is impossible to stitch two dissimilar things together).

7 *Meng'asunoyu olkesen etioyo en-kerai* – Don't make a cloth for carrying a child before the child is born (one should never plan ahead on how to spend the money earned from any project, before the outcome of any such effort).

8 *E-te-jo olg'ojine me a-ke amunyak keju naagol* – The hyena said it is not that I have luck, but my leg is strong (meaning I have luck it is true, but I also have to work).

9 *E-baiki enkutuk nainosa isunya neinos in-kik; nebaiki enainosa nkik neinos isunya!* – It is possible that the mouth that ate fat can also eat excreta and that which ate excreta shall eat fat!

(A rich person can be overcome by misfortunes till he is completely poor; and a poor person can strike a fortune overnight or win a lottery and be as rich! What goes up must come down and vice versa!)

10 *Meshetai en-kang' nagilita e-nopeny* – Literal translation: One cannot build a house which the owner is breaking ! (Meaning that it is impossible to save a marriage when both people have reached a point of no return and are not ready to compromise!)

MAASAI RIDDLES

Maasai riddles (*il-oyiotiaa*) are introduced as follows: – (Here is a riddle – *Oyiote* – The reply is *Eeuo* (It has come)

1 *Balbal tenkusero?* A pool in the plain?
Answer: *Emudong Oltome!* The elephant's Placenta!

71

2   *Eikirnyanya minyi tol-tiren?* Your father is struggling/ making great efforts in the sitting room?
Answer: *O-coni okititoi.* A hide being scraped to remove hairs using a small hand axe.

3   *Ejo ropirrop e puoita idia alo nejo kumkum epuonu ena alo?* Lit. Trans. What is loud in one direction and quiet in the other?
Answer: *Inkurkurto naayai enkare!* The calabashes taken for drawing water!

4   *Dorrop en-tito ai neyiolo atushuma kule?* My daughter is short but she knows how to keep milk?
Answer: *Olotori.* A bee.

5   *Euno parkilai te boo?* A rocking movement in the Kraal?
Answer: *Osinkolio!* A dance!

6   *Tamanai tele doinyo nimikitumo aikata?* Go to this direction of the mountain and I to the other and we shall never meet?
Answer: *Inkiyiaa!* Ears!

7. *Eijululo nemepuo?* They bend but do not discharge?
Answer: *Ilki loo nkishu!* The cow's tits!

8   *Ashomo enda ang' etuateki nalo aye?* When I went to that home and found people dead, I also died?
Answer: *Ashomo ainepu iltung'anak eirurate nalo sii nanu airura!* I went and found them asleep and I slept also.

9   *Iyiopiyopa ele reyiet ing'oru ngutunyi nangelaa?* Go down this river and look for your teasing mother?
Answer: *Entamejoi!* Nettle!

10 *Eado ngutunyi nemebaiki enkoshoke enker?* Your mother is tall but she cannot reach the sheep's stomach?
Answer: *Enk-oitoi.* The pathway.

11 *Ening'o mukumper toldonyo?* A splitting sound is heard on the hill?
Answer: *Entolu.* An axe.

12   *Meidimu isirkon oong'uan?* Four asses cannot afford?
Answer: *Emuro enkalaoni!* The thigh of an ant.

13   *Epuo loleteyio omeimiso ilkidong'o?* Messes Loleteyio go
       with flickering tails?
Answer: *Ilkeek le nkima!* The firewoods!

14   *Inyo te ine matotona?* What is it?
Answer: *Erashe musana eng'ejuk.* The old and the new
       patch.

15   *Ol-murrani lai' odo kutuk?* My warrior with red lips?
Answer: *Ol-ng'oret!* Arrowhead. (The arrow for bleeding
       cattle, usually pointed at one end and feathered at
       the other, for shooting from a bow.)

16   *E-man e-nkiu te siare?* It goes around the anthill with a
       club?
Answer: *E-motonyi naitaapa ilayiok!* A bird impregnated
       by the boys!

17   *Airriwayie nelo pii?* I send and went for good?
Answer: *Embeneyioi nawa enkare.* The leaf taken away by
       water!

18   *Timini nkuume?* I think of a funny nose?
Answer: *Enkume enkalaoni!* The nose of an ant!

19   *Oo nipi nimintieu atotonie entito e Kirkoris endukuya?*
       Though you are brave, do you dare to sit on the head
       of Kilkoris girl?
Answer: *Ermet!* A spear!

20   *Eiduraki te nkang' neing'uari enkaina enkitok ai?* Moved
       from a home and the hand of my wife is left behind?
Answer: *Olarao eika too rishina!* (Small piece of leather
       used as a broom in the calves' pen.) Hanging on the
       post!

21   *Sii – sii?* Something that causes one to wonder?
Answer: A longing for the fruits that I cannot reach!
       Meaning the heights and heights I cannot reach!

22 *Ijo keishiraki te dukuya nekua kishu nemeishiri oshi ake?* People are screaming in front of those cattle and they do not scream always?
Answer: *Olojong'ani loo ntorosi.* The leg of the brave fly is broken.

23 *Neliido nele?* There it is, here it is?
Answer: *Oloijiliai le kule!* The drop of milk!

24 *Tinka narikito tinka nadung'o tinka?* Tinka leading Tinka with a cut?
Answer: *Esikiria narikito enkurraru nadung'o kiyiaa!* A donkey leading a colt with ears cut!

25 *Ijo eewuo?* You say it comes?
Answer: *Enkiroroto ai o enino!* My words with yours!

26 *Iyopiyopare ele reyiet ing'oru il-aras le minyi?* Go along this river and look for the ribs of your father?
Answer: *Il-abur le nkare.* The water foam.

27 *Amburrlulu?* An opening in the wall?
Answer: *Elusie enkaji.* The window of the hut/house.

28 *Edung' ng'utunyi olosinko e-rumisho enebanji?* Your mother crosses the cattle pen with a protruding part of this size?
Answer: *En-keju en-kerai.* The child's foot.

29 *Epong'a minyi tol-tiren?* Your father is constipated in the sitting room?
Answer: *E-moti oo naishi!* A pot of brew!

30 *Sikirai tioitoi?* A shell at the path?
Answer: *En-kanyarati!* Spittle!

31 *Edung' ng'utunyi olosinko e-mukita enapiak?* Your mother is crossing the cattle pen with her mouth full?
Answer: *En-kimujati!* Soaked tobacco! (Holding tobacco between cheek and gum to absorb nicotine.)

32 *Eidurraki te nkang' neshukunye ol-kine ng'iro ol-muate?* People immigrated and the khaki he-goat returned to the kraal?
Answer: *En-terit!* Dust!

33 *Enak il-asho laainei meimiso il-kidong'o?* My calves suck
    until their tails disappear?
    Answer: *Il-keek le-nkima!* Firewood

34 *Aata il-murran lainei okuni nemedung'o enking'uana metii
    oliokuni?* I have three warriors but they do not decide
    in the meeting when the third one is not present?
    Answer: *Isoito le nkima!* The stones of the fire! (The
    stones for standing the cooking pot on at the fire; the
    pot cannot be balanced on two stones so the third
    one is absolutely necessary: a discussion too is not
    resolved if only two people take part in it.)

Niani helped her grandmother (her father's mother)
most of the evenings during her school holidays especially to
pull the *ol-tim* or *o-logol* and later to close the *en-kishomi* (gate)
with additional dry branches until it was the same level as the
gate post. The *ol-tim* or *o-logol* is usually one piece of wood
made with many branches of *ol-orien*. The closing of the gate
is usually done as soon as the sun went down immediately
after the return of cows from their grazing. The *en-kishomi*
is closed to ensure their protection from attacks from wild
animals. While the adult cows remain in the *e-mboo* after they
have been milked, their young ones are then separated from
them. After that, Naini would bring the calves into the calves'
pen (*olale*), which was usually within the same hut.

Most evenings, after dinner, the old ladies chewed *ol-kimbau* (tobacco) mixed with *emakat* (soda ash) while spitting
the brown stuff from time to time (*anotaa inkamulak ol-kimbau*. The tobacco was usually kept in the *ol-kirau/ol-kidong*
tobacco container by most of the Maasai elders both women
and men. For those who took *en-kisugi*, like Naini's mother,
she kept it in an *entulet* (snuff container). Naini used to go to
the local market to buy her grandmother *ol-kimbau*.

There was also a sheep pen (*e-muatat oo ntare*). She would
also close the door of the pen, then thereafter the main door
of the hut with *orike*, which is some sort of doormat made
from woven thickly tangled green twigs used in the late night
to close off the entrance leading into the main hut. Two bars

75

are placed upright on the middle of the entrance leaning on the door mat. To fasten it, two more small bars are placed across one another into the door poles that serve as door frames.

In the morning, Naini swept the floor of the calves' pen with *o-larao*, a small piece of leather which served as a broom to brush off the cow dung and the calves' urine from the pot-holes in the *ola le*. After that she swept it with some grass (*e-woret*). This method of cleaning was used and is still used as the floors are not cemented, but soil. She then took the calves' dung to the kraal (*e-mboo*) and added it to the dung-hill (*ol-chala*) which is inside the homestead. The Maasai village was laid out in a circle surrounded by a hedge made of twigs and thorns. The *enkang* inside the kraal is a homestead occupied by several elders with their wives and children and possibly some grandparents.

Huts were made from grass, twigs and cowdung. The mud-thatched roofs were frequently repaired, especially during the rainy season to avoid any leakage. This was done using fresh cow dung. All the same, a typical Maasai hut always had an *erishina*, which is a straight strong pole that serves as support for the roof. After going to secondary school, on Sundays, the students always went to the AIC Church, which was about two miles from the school. On the way, the students always stopped at a *mukahawa* (restaurant) to buy some doughnuts.

As they walked across the small stream at the shopping centre, towards the church, Naini's friend Neliyio invited her to the *mukahawa* for a cup of tea. Since they were only allowed a few minutes to stop by, Naini took her cup of tea hurriedly, using a saucer to save time by pouring it into it so as to cool it quickly ... at the same time eating her piece of bread and butter. This particular incident reminded her of her grandmother's tea back home, when she could exhale air to make a slight breeze to blow through her big mug of tea several times so as to reduce the steam in it. At home, she often poured her tea back and forth into a pot then returned it once again to the cup. This method was faster than using the saucer. This she did repeatedly, one hand holding the cup, the other holding the pot making some sort of stream with the brownish tea.

After her grandmother had boiled it, mixing both the milk and water, she would then add tea leaves and sugar, then pour it through the strainer.

The recollection made Naini's mouth water for a cup of home-made tea, with that special flavour.

Neliyio reminded Naini that it was time to leave for church. They hurried to catch up with the rest of the girls before it was noticed that they were lagging behind, which would cause them a problem with the school matron. As they entered the church, Naini thanked Neliyio for the entertainment.

At their very first meeting, they developed a friendship and this has never ceased. Since her home was not so far from school as Naini's, most of the time when Neliyio's parents brought her food, she would invite Naini to share it. Naini remembers the day when they could not find water to make tea or chocolate, she could mix sugar with dry cocoa and they ate it.

As they went to have a shower together for the first time, Naini noticed that her friend had a black mark on her back. Not knowing that it was a birthmark, Naini started to scrub her back until the skin peeled off. She then assured her that it had disappeared! It was not until it started to bleed that Naini realized that she had hurt her. This was not all; the following day, it was nearly impossible for her to wear clothes. That night she could hardly sleep because of pain. Naini had done that to her chocolate skin in order to get rid of her skin disease, due to her ignorance in not knowing that Neliyio had been born with it. It made Naini very sad to see her friend suffering, but she did not blame herself for it because she was also happy that it had disappeared!

During their stay at the boarding school, Neliyio became a girlfriend of one of Naini's relatives who was in the same school, so Naini became the postman taking the letters to him and bringing back the replies to her.

After circumcision, Neliyio returned to school before she was completely cured. When the female teacher commanded her to run, she told her she was incapable as she was still sick after circumcision. Since this particular teacher had never been circumcised, she couldn't understand the pains Naini's friend was still passing through. So, to support her, Naini also refused to do the sports during that period until she was completely cured.

Although teacher Sharon was expected to be understanding and to respect the girls, she completely refused to let them rest. So they went to inform the matron, an elderly lady with great understanding who in turn requested permission on their behalf. As a result of this, although the teacher had agreed to forgive Naini and her friend after the matron had intervened by requesting her not to put them on hard labour. The teacher did not honour her word. She still assigned them manual work far from the dormitory. This incident, of returning to school before being completely cured after circumcision reminded Naini of Primary School, where a similar incident happened to a newly circumcised girl who returned to do her written examination test followed by practical tests in 1958 in her ceremonial attire of *enkaibartani*. She won great admiration from the public and many compliments of her determination for success. The teachers were happy to have her in the examination room despite her not being completely cured. Nadupa passed her examination but unfortunately, like many others, she was married away by her family not long after that.

6

CIRCUMCISION

It was during her third term holidays that Naini was informed that they were preparing for her circumcision together with the other girls of her age in their village. She was not surprised by this outcome as it was the clan's decision that determined when and where the occasion ought to take place. The young were expected to abide by their commands.

Circumcision preparation commences about one month before the date calculated according to the moon (*isopiain*). The person/s intending to circumcise his/their daughters would then go round informing all those who would take part in the preparation.

The families concerned gather all the pots needed for the occasion, even those available at distance villages. The people of the village always join together to help in any of these communal activities such as those of removing the maize grains from the maize cobs. To hasten the process of removing them from their cobs, we put them inside a large sisal bag then use a stick to thresh them, having tied the open end of the bag. Maize is a cereal plant with the grains borne on cobs enclosed in husks. The type we grow in Kenya with big white seeds is the particular one used for brewing.

After the grains are dried in the sun they are ground into flour at the windmill.

Then comes *enukata o-lmanyua* – fermenting the corn flour – and later *aisus* – frying/roasting it over an open fire using charcoal until it is all brown in colour. The respective families would then meet to decide where the event would take place and at whose home, if there were several girls being circumcised. When *ol-mayua* is ready, it is then dried in the sun for several days and kept ready for the occasion in bags in a dry place.

In the meantime, they also prepare the millet (*aitubulu i-mumerek*), fermenting it too for the occasion. After fermentation, it is then dried for several days. This is later ground with a grinding stone until it is fine flour. The *i-mumerek* and *ol-mayua* are then mixed together, put in the pots then filled with cold water to brew – *aamuk*. The *inaishi* is at this stage more like the porridge. To hasten the process off fermentation, the pots are placed round the fireplace. During the entire brewing period the fire is constantly lit in the huts where the pots of brew are. It is usually ready by the eve of the occasion. A bracelet of grass supports and steadies the clay pot during the brewing period and also when drinking *inaishi* from it, using wooden straws (*enkiseketi*).

All the invited guests come to the home carrying their own *enkiseketi* for communal drinking of the *inaishi*, which is sipped whilst the drinker is a distance away from *emoti* – the pot – which is usually kept in the centre of the room during the drinking period.

Aen e-moti is the ceremony of tying the drinking pot soon after circumcision. This is done by the elders, who are normally of the same age group as the girl's father. It is symbolized by tying *e-sinandei* and the Kikuyu grass *e-naimuruai* around the neck of the earthenware pot. The first to do so will give a heifer to the girl's father, while the second person will give an ox. This is done ceremoniously to signify that the girl met all her early obligations and the father is happy.

The family members start arriving as early as three days before the day of the ceremony. Other visitors come a day or so before the circumcision day. Most of them come with gifts. Beer, honey, milk and even goats.

The day before the circumcision day is usually a very busy one. Everyone wakes up early in preparation for the arriving visitors. Food has to be cooked and water drawn from the nearby river. This occasion is a great one and everyone in the village would participate in one thing or the other. Two and even sometimes three cows would be slaughtered, depending on how rich the family is, and roasted over fires lit in the open with *il-jepeta* using skewers. This is done by men while women boil the meat. The intestines and the other internal parts such as *e-nkaya, enaingoring'orisho,* are selected and washed in the stream by women. The intestines are squeezed – *aalep imonyit.* Also prepared is *monono,* a Maasai dish made from fresh blood, fat and meat fried together. The other special dish for the occasion that is prepared for the newly circumcised girl is *ol-purda.* The liver is given to expectant mothers and it is eaten raw when it is still fresh and warm. The heart and the kidneys can not be preserved as there is no refrigeration available so it is also eaten on the same day. The meat to be kept for future consumption is prepared very fast to prevent it from rotting. Preserving meat is a Maasai tradition from time immemorial.

Blood and fats are drained out, leaving only the lean meat. This is then spread and cut into straight ropes known as *i-sirikan* (biltong), which are stored in one big room hung like clothes after being steeped in salty water. They are dried for several days until they are dry as firewood, then removed and preserved in *e-noos* – a wooden container or any other container for later use. This kind of meat can be kept for a very long time without becoming stale and so is the *olpurda.* In later use, *i-sirikan* can be boiled or roasted over a charcoal fire. In some cases, the meat is beaten with a stone to make it soft (*a-wosh-iosh to soit*). This is a Maasai delicacy. After eating this kind of meat, one should have plenty of water to drink. It is very filling and nourishing, taking into account the way it is prepared and preserved with its juices. This kind of meat is mainly preserved for the dry season when milk is not enough to drink. Unfortunately, this practice is slowly fading away as the Maasai people have now started growing all types of foodstuff. This is also the case because most people don't own refrigerators. One, because they are expensive. Two, due to lack of electricity in the remote areas.

Ol purda – meat preserved in fat – can also be kept for a

very long time. This is a mixture of melted fat and lean meat cooked in soft fats without adding any water. This is mostly administered to nursing mothers and *enkaibartak*, and also to those recovering from illness. Naini enjoyed eating both dishes during the ceremony and during her stay as *enkaibartani*, after circumcision.

The rest of the meat, like the head, the tongue and hooves *iloilelek* – are scorched over a glowing fire to burn away the fur, and then used to make soup. Soup is usually drunk by all and the heart is eaten by the father and his contemporaries. Nothing is wasted, including the bones removed from *i-sirikan* – they are also used to make soup.

DRYING THE COW'S HIDE – *OL-CHONI/ENDAPANA*

The skin of the slaughtered cow would be placed on a flat surface and by the use of *incheito* sharpened on one side (small wooden peggings) fastened to the ground, the sharpened sides facing the ground and passed through small holes made all along the sides of the hide, the inside facing upwards. Then, with a kitchen knife, all the fat and meat is removed and left to dry.

The hide (*ol-choni*) is later used as a bedspread after it has been properly treated (*aak it*) and the hair removed using a knife or a small axe (especially designed for this purpose), after which it is oiled till it is smooth. It is then placed on top of a bundle of dry grass known as *isisineti* which serves as a mattress. This tradition is still practised in most of the Maasai homes upcountry. Naini describes this bedding as comfortable especially when used on the traditional Maasai permanent beds – *e-ruat* – in the countryside. This type of bed is made of four wooden poles (*il kipereri*) and branches placed across the bed and tied in place with *inkopit* strings. Within the Maasai house the two beds are erected opposite each other with the fire place in between them. The footside always faces the fire. One bed is for the woman and the children and the other for the husband. The bedroom side is enclosed as there is a partition between the *olale* (calves' pen) and the bedroom, which is also the fire place.

Each season before the rains start, normally during the months of March through to May, the women gather firewood to last through the rainy period, and to avoid going to the forest because of the dangers of crawling insects and reptiles due to the tall grass and dew. In the afternoons of the rainy season the women sit together doing the handicrafts, such as decoration of *inkurkurtok* – calabashes/gourds – and *isioten* and beadwork.

A typical fire place is made by placing three big water stones of the same size in a triangular layout round a hole dug in the ground, leaving enough space in between them for firewood – *isoito le nkima* (literal translation: stone of the fire). This hole is plastered with a mixture of soil and water and the surface finished and smoothed by smearing a cover of cow dung. This finish is re-dressed occasionally to prevent cracks.

When one is cooking using a small pot, a smaller stone is added on one side of the fire for adjustment. This type of fire is always lit using firewood which comprises twigs plus a big log of wood – *o-leng'oti.*

The Maasai original house is the *manyatta* type but nowadays they have adapted to the modern house from their long-term neighbours and trading partners the Kalenjin. The bedroom has a temporary door and it is separated from the sitting room – *oltiren* – and they now have *oltapot*, the kiln in the ceiling made from sticks where firewood is kept to dry.

INAISHI

The drinking of the *inaishi* began the previous evening soon after the arrival of the relatives and a few guests. The folks continued drinking *inaishi* with their straws from the clay pots, and when it became a bit too thick to pass through the straws, then warm water was added to dilute it to the consistency that could flow through the *inkiseketi*. The warming of the water and the adding of firewood was mainly done in turns by the ladies.

The visitors, especially the female ones, for their contributions, brought milk, eggs, maize flour for cooking *ugali* (maize porridge), firewood to be used during the occasion and water. The majority brought water as it was a necessity for the occasion and most of all, because there was no tap water in the area.

For such a ceremony, some people travelled long distances, stones burning under their feet like hot coal, but still kept going on. Even the two-month-olds endured the hundred miles strapped onto their mothers' backs; they could not be left out of this great occasion. It definitely was a great occasion with plenty of free food and drinks. By the end of the first evening many youngsters were fast asleep, exhausted from the long journeys. There was a lot of singing and dancing going on. The girls who were going to be circumcised with Naini the following day all wore *il-pirrirrin* (bells) designed by the blacksmith (*il-kunono*) especially for such occasions, which were tied to their thighs and produced beautiful sounds whenever the wearer moved.

There are four types of *il-pirrirrin*. One large and one small are worn on each leg. The main ones used by girls are oblong in shape and made of iron and the clappers are round like bullets. The outfits were usually painted red with ochres and their necks adorned with beads and their ears fitted with *imuna* for the young ones, the Maasai local earrings.

Naini and the other girls danced forward and backwards in a row, facing the warriors, while singing ceremonial songs led by the best singer. *Il-pirrirrin* were tied to their thighs. In turn they sang while moving their bodies, especially their thighs to shake the *il-pirrirrin* at the same time swinging the fly-whisks (*il-kidongo*) which were made from the long hairs of the wildebeest *il-enyok lo-inkat* in the air, higher and higher. There were many dancers all dressed in elegant attire and with lots of ornaments. In the singing, the words used were mostly those of praise, especially of one's cows and the raids he made in the past. The young men and the young girls danced together in rhythm. In these vigorous dances, young men exhibited their style and strength by jumping as high as they could with their clubs and spears. They leapt from the ground, up and down, while the young ladies and young girls shouted words of praise and of love.

It was while dancing with the warriors on this particular evening in preparation for her circumcision day, that Naini remembered the famous inter-schools music festival that took her to Nairobi for the first time, accompanying a group, which cost her all her pocket money! It was on one early morning that we boarded a bus that was ordered for us by the headmaster in conjunction with the choir master, Mr Ole Kenini, who was to accompany us throughout the trip as he was the conductor. To Naini's excitement, she was included in the trip, which was going to take them to a big city.

Unlike their usual trip in the lorry, the bus seats were more comfortable, with many windows which permitted them to see the countryside. After a long drive, since Naini was by the window, she tried to sit up. She was feeling dizzy because the bus was speeding away and the trees, the grass, the road were moving backwards. She started feeling nausea. A girl she was sitting with told her to shut her eyes, and they changed positions. After a while, Naini was fast asleep.

As they arrived near Mount Longonot, Naisimoi woke her up just in time. The choir master was saying they would soon arrive at the tarmac road, at the junction of the Nairobi/Naivasha roads. Naini in turn asked the girl what a tarmac road was like; she told her it was a road which had been cemented with murrum. But Naisimoi knew better than the first girl because she came from Ngong. She objected to that and then explained that it was a road paved with crushed stones and tar.

When they arrived in Nairobi, they were driven directly to the Kenya National theatre hall. By this time most of the other groups were already seated. It was a colourful ceremony, children dressed in different kind of uniforms. Naini's group was dressed in their khaki uniforms. It was number five in the list to perform that morning. They quietly left their benches and proceeded to the stage. By the time their performance ended, it was nearly the end of the afternoon.

For their good performance, teacher Ole Kenini decided to take them for a city tour since he knew that many students had never been to the capital and might never set foot in the near future, especially the girls who would be married off. They went to River Road as this area was considered cheaper than the rest of the shops. Naini had always wanted to buy herself a pair of shoes. For this trip, her uncle had given her a lump sum of money, five shillings, which was a lot of money then.

With the help of her fellow students, Naini managed to choose a pair. As she was trying on the shoes, in order to have both her hands free, she placed the piece of cloth which served as her purse on top of the shop counter. The shoes fitted very well! By this time, all eyes were on her new pair of shoes. With admiration, Naisimoi said how she wished she could also buy a pair. As Naini stood up to pay for them, the piece of cloth had disappeared! She couldn't believe her eyes. They all searched for it in vain. Their teacher, who was busy shopping himself, came to help them look for it. He immediately knew that it was stolen.

Naini was then told by the shopkeeper to remove the shoes if she had no other money to pay for them. While she was removing the shoes, tears rolled down her cheeks to the cemented floor. As she returned the shoes to the shopkeeper, tears rolled onto her khaki uniform. She wiped them with the back of her hand as she had no handkerchief to use. The piece of cloth which she had just lost together with the money also served as her handkerchief. She was struck by the fact that the loss of the only money she had did not only prevent her possessing the shoes but also deprived her of any other comfort, entertainment and most of all her meals for the next few days.

Even to this day, Naini really doesn't know who stole her money, whether it was the shopkeeper, a student or just a town thief. How foolish I was to have kept the money on top of the counter, she thought. After all these years, she has never forgotten this incident as it was very painful to lose that kind of money when she needed it most.

At that instant, one of the women organizers came up to her to ask why she wasn't dancing any more. Naini just went on to relate to her what has distracted her mind about that incident. She was relieved to learn that it was something else and that it was not about their awaited circumcision. She was frank with her, as she said, 'I had thought you were planning to escape the operation!'

After that, Naini joined the rest of the girls once again in dancing.

Throughout the night while the singing went on, others roasted meat on the hot burning flames of the fire. Meat was usually roasted using *il-jepeta* (skewers) in the moonlight.

Very late in the night, the girls who were going to be circumcised were separated from the young men and general crowd (*ol–orere*) for the closed-doors ceremonies.

By this time, most of the old folks had fallen asleep long before sunset due to fatigue and drinking alcohol, but some old-timers continued drinking *inaishi* using their straws while listening to the songs and joining quietly in the singing, uttering the few words they could remember and reflecting back on their youth and all the best memories of their times.

The following day before sunrise, the girls and the female organizers left the home, heading for the river. The girls took a quick wash at the river bank then soon after they returned to the village. By this time, the operational area was already prepared and sealed for females only and the *enkamuratani*, the female circumciser, was ready with her sharp knife, *ol-murunya*, to perform the painful operation. When Naini sat down to be examined by the old ladies, they were happy to learn that Naini was still a virgin, this was a cause for great pride to her family. Customarily before circumcision, all the girls are made to sit on a backless four-legged stool with no arms (*olorika loo nkejek ong'uan*). On it is fresh cream and some green grass (*eng'orno olperes*). A girl who had lost her virginity would not undergo this process, causing great embarrassment to the family concerned as this is witnessed by everyone. This is why during 'moranship', the warriors always abstain from having sexual intercourse with the young girls

87

during the time they were together at *olpul* to avoid breaking the young girls' virginity. The moran has to exercise so much self-control that he can even sleep between the girl's legs (*ajing polos oo inkupesin*) and restrain himself from being overcome by his emotions! They are quite disciplined.

After Naini and the rest came back from the river, and went through the above formalities, the lady circumciser appeared. As soon as she sat down, her knife was ready at hand – she then uncovered and parted Naini's thighs and her tiny slim legs and immediately cut part of her private parts, removing her clitoris *olopide* and the *labia minora.*

During the operation, they were all seated on a skin in a row, having one common support and the same knife was used on all of them. There were no pain-killers used. The knife was so sharp that Ng'oto Nairuko cut each girl's clitoris once and it was over! She was so quick that some women organizers re-checked the girls after the operation before paying her for services rendered, doubting her swiftness, but to her disbelief all were perfectly done. In Naini's group, none of the girls was a coward (*ema-kuetai*). On such occasions, it was surprising and amazing how the news spread as fast as bush fire. News such as how a girl screamed during circumcision (*ema-kuetai*) or of a girl who had become pregnant before circumcision (a taboo – in Kimaasai *e-ntaapai*). But such cases were rare if any at all. If a girl gets pregnant before being circumcised, the family will then wait until the baby has been born. It is then done the same day, soon after delivery. Circumsision is never done when the girl is pregnant because the mother might faint during the exercise, causing harm to the unborn child.

During circumcision, nearly all the clan elders gather for this very festive celebration (*e-masho*) and contribute to its success in any way they deem helpful, except of course those who were unable to come due to other commitments or due to illness and old age. Usually soon after circumcision, if all went as planned, women raised a war cry '*aa-rua – ariri-ririi*' till they fainted as a way of letting out steam from the excitement and pride to announce that all was well.

During the entire exercise, one had to be brave, not to twist a muscle or even blink or worse still not to scream as this indicated a cowardice, which caused great embarrassment to the family and whole clan. Naini's face, as well as the faces of those who were circumcised together were closely watched by the surrounding women. The brave girls were rewarded with bundles of *e-sinandei*, the tree of milk, or *olcani le NkA* (*Podocarpus milanjianus*) and other presents, e.g. bangles, beads from the murans and a heifer from the father.

During Naini's youth, uncircumcised girls were few if any as most families during that time took circumcision seriously, even those who adhered to the church, as it meant a break-through between childhood and adulthood for both boys and girls.

One of the girls who was circumcised with Naini bled pro-fusely till she fainted. After circumcision, Naini and the rest were dressed in black beaded hide robes and decorative chains before being led away to recuperate. As *inkaibartak*, their faces were enveloped in some kind of masks. The masks were also made of leather and they stayed at *olale loo inkaibartak*, a seclusion area. As was usual the group had a young girl assigned to bring them food and who also ate with them. The young girl served as a guide whenever they wanted to go somewhere. They wore this attire till the final ceremonies were performed once again, amidst more brewing of alcohol. Alcohol was brewed again when Naini was being released so that she could go back to school.

During the whole period when Naini was *enkaibartani*, her mother kept her hair *ol-masi* until after Naini was shaved when she was initiated. Women are supposed to keep their hair after circumcising their daughters. This hair (the *ol-masi*) on the head signifies a person's special status as the one mentioned above. This is also the case after childbirth.

While some people were busy with the circumcision events, others were busy taking part in other activities, such as slaughtering the cow for the feast. The man of the home-stead would take a rope, a bow and one blunted arrow. Assisted by other members of the family he would tie the neck of the cow and then obtain blood by piercing and bleeding the cow through the jugular vein. This blood is mixed with fresh milk and drunk by the *inkaibartak* and the whole family after removing *elimanet*.

The visitors continued drinking *inaishi* to celebrate as now the time for the people to make merry had come. Some were already drunk after drinking the whole night long. Since there was not much else to do, they continued drinking, with a few joining in the dancing and singing from time to time.

Ng'oto Nairuko and the other women organizers of the ceremony who could not drink as much the night before, so as to keep watch of every activity taking place, took to their fill to celebrate their success. This went on for over three days in all. Many of her friends sang in praise of Ng'oto Nairuko for her good performance. Soon after circumcision, the visitors started leaving the home especially those with small children who were left behind.

Afterwards, the same morning, Naini and the rest of the *inkaibartak* were given some milk and blood mixture as this was easy to digest. By this time, they were in so much pain that they could not even enjoy the delicious drink. The pain was so acute that every one of them was near tears. The bleeding had become worse for some. The first three days were worst of all. Naini could hardly walk because of the wound. Passing urine was a nightmare, it burnt so badly that she dreaded drinking anything, wanting to avoid going to urinate or even pass a stool.

She had to wash her private parts with salty warm water as this was the only remedy for their healing. It relieved the pain and soon the wounds were nearly cured. Two weeks later, she could even run without much difficulty. Soon all her pains were long forgotten. It was quite an experience!

During the healing time after circumcision, they were kept busy through lessons on design and sewing of *olekesena*, a leather garment for wrapping around a lady's waist made from goat's hide (*en-dapana*). The *olekesena* is usually decorated with beads using a sinew (*e-mpito*) to string up the beads together. They also learnt how to join the pieces of leather

90

together to make *olekesena lol-cholo*. The special dress *olekesena* is worn mostly on special occasions and is worn below the waistline with another piece on the upper part.

It was also during this period that Naini learned how to make most of the beadwork, including how to decorate the calabashes or gourds and to sew on the leather pieces which serve as straps on the calabash *aripaki i-nkeenta i-nkurkurtok*.

Boys and girls are circumcised according to the Maasai traditions. For the girls it is usually between the ages of 12 and 13 years. They remain initiated as *inkaibartak* until when they have been completely cured. The period can last up to a year, the *inkaibartak* being specially fed and do not see men.

From this time on Naini was no longer considered a girl but as a young unmarried woman known in Kimaasai as *e-siankiki*.

The final brewing ceremony was scheduled for the end of December, just before Naini resumed school.

The rest of the *inkaibartak* remained for several months thereafter as they were not attending school. As for Naini, the ceremony of shaving her head was done a month after circumcision to initiate her *a-barn*. Another word used and which means the same ceremony is *a-bolu e-ntito*, meaning to set the girl free, while the word *a-barn* means to shave during a special occasion. Usually after this occasion, the young ladies wore their *ilokesenani* and their ceremonial ornaments (*imasaa*) as indicated earlier on. Naini's case was a unique one as she was the only one being set free before the rest to enable her to go to school.

Besides all these ceremonies and all that took place within this short time, Naini was already looking forward to going back to school and once again meeting her other friends. She longed to go back and continue with her education.

Traditionally, soon after the initiation ceremony the marriage takes place. Unlike the men, girls have no age limits even though for them there are rules governing which age group they should marry and to which clan. The main reason for this is to avoid any mistakes of intermarriages of children coming from the same clan or within relatives. In order to be

91

considered, the qualification of the man depends entirely on his background and that of his family. On the other hand, a girl who was a virgin and was brave and bold during circumcision is highly respected.

Usually after the above criteria have been satisfied, most girls are thereafter given away.

7

NAINI'S MARRIAGE

Once in school, Naini knew she would have to work hard to achieve a good position in class by the end of the beginning year, otherwise Lemiso would refuse to pay her school fees. As it was, she was in a way lucky that she was at least allowed to go back to school after circumcision even though only for another two terms.

Today, circumcision of girls – called female genital mutilation – is forbidden by the authorities even though people still practise it secretly as the Maasai believe that any uncircumcised person is not grown-up.

During Naini's absence at the boarding school, Tim's family went to her parents' home to declare their interest, that their son wanted to marry Naini. All was discussed and they were informed to await the final decision after Naini's arrival from her school at Narok. They then left as agreed.

Before this proposal, during circumcision, many other families had proposed to marry Naini, but her father did not accept any proposal as he had wanted to let her continue with her education, as was originally discussed and agreed by the two brothers Lomunyak and Lemiso. Naini had then continued with her education in Narok for nearly three years without interruption.

On arrival from Narok school, she was informed that Tim's family had been there to declare their interest and that she would soon be married. Tim came with another man to see her father some days before, but she did not know the reason for their visit, even though she was told later by a friend who had seen them during the first occasion and who had overheard their conversation.

It was then that Naini realized that things had taken a dramatic turn as she knew that she might not go to school as was originally planned! Her family had then agreed to marry her off, due to the fact that Tim's family were from the Iloibonok, and so they believed that if they refused to marry her to Tim, some misfortune would befall them. Above all, one thing was sure, Tim's family were known for their herds of cattle and this was also taken into consideration as it guaranteed Naini's comfort and assured that she would live in good conditions.

Naini then remembered that the man who came to her father's home accompanying Tim had also attended the same school when she joined standard five at Narok secondary school and left at the end of the same year.

The arrangements were done so hurriedly that within a period of one week, all the preparations were completed. Although some of the traditions were observed, Naini was not shown her cows neither was she given the usual presents and, unlike her sister, she was not dressed in the leather garment *olekesena*. Her sister Nareyro's marriage was a full Maasai traditional one and she stayed the usual four days with her mother-in-law while trying to get accustomed to her new home and surroundings. Naini's marriage was not the same.

Naini's husband, Tim was born of the *Iloibonok* family. He too had been to school. Born in a rich family, Tim would not take anything seriously. He got all he wanted whenever he asked from his parents. He was 6 feet tall and of light complexion. Tim was much older than Naini. His father had four wives: Tim's mother was the second one and the one most loved by her husband (*enkirotet*). Tim was the fourth born of Ole Leparakuo. His mother is Kitaana.

Ole Leparakuo's family was large compared to the rest of the families living at Elang'ata O Saen – literal translation, the valley of beads. Unlike the rest of the family, Tim's father was very kind to Naini, which was the opposite to Tim's

94

mother. There was no single time that she invited Naini to go to the village to identify the cows she was given. Had she been a good mother she could have guided Naini to that effect, and also guided her on how to run the home.

The marriage issue was a great shock to her but she was too young to argue or to even try and defend herself, but at least she tried. She insisted that she wanted to continue with her education but this cry fell on deaf ears. Her adoptive father told her there was no way she was going to continue with school. If she wanted, he had told her, as an option, she would ask her husband to pay for her school fees for the remaining period of her studies. Naini is still bitter about this as she was just a little girl. The option he gave her was an impossible one. How could she go to school and at the same time run a home. There was no secondary school she could go to in her home area even if she wanted and she doubted if the man would have let her go to her former school in Narok!

Being so young, she did not see any way to solve her problem. Perhaps she could have reasoned it out, if only she was of age. She could have gone to a family planning centre but it was non-existent in her home area at that time, they could have helped her. It is a pity that there were no such facilities then. Although she was then too young to think about this, she now doubts if the man could have allowed her anyway. She is certain that the man would have declined her request and that could have added more disappointments to her sad childhood.

After the arrangements of the marriage, Naini was then taken the following evening, and the same night, that man forced her to sleep with him against her will. She had never had any sexual experience before. It all started that very night at the tender age of 13 going on 14 years. It was very hard for her and from that incident, she developed hatred towards men due to this bad experience. By her fourteenth birthday, she was already put in the family way.

During her pregnancy she underwent a lot of mistreatment from that family – unlike her sister Nareyro, whose marriage followed the usual Maasai traditional way of marriage, and who stayed with her mother-in-law for the four days as a custom while trying to get accustomed to her new home and surroundings.

8

MAASAI WEDDINGS

Child bride or child marriage is a phenomenon that is still practised in some parts of Kenya, especially among communities in the NEP and Rift Valley Province. This practice dates from time immemorial, and it is time it was brought to an end for the welfare of future generations.

According to Maasai culture, Naini feels, it does not promote moral justice and because of its insubstantial role in society, this practice tends to frustrate and hinder the intellectual from advancement. Naini admits that we must keep some of our cultures and norms and values but it is spine-chilling for a girl under age to be forced into marriage to an older man even older than her own father, as a fifth or even sixth wife. As she looks back now, Naini remembers some of the girls of her youth *in-toyie esirit enye* who grew up with her and who managed only to learn up to standard two or three, who are now old women with large families and living very difficult lives. Due to childbearing, and a heavy workload, they have prematurely aged and that is not all, they can neither read nor write as the moment they were given away, they left everything behind, as they couldn't cope with the hardships that surrounded them. This is very sad. They gave up due to frustration or perhaps because of bringing up their children with more or less nothing. It was felt that the place for a woman was the kitchen, and they were made to believe it.

Due to lack of education and pressure from the community, they have completely neglected themselves in fulfilling the demands of their dead ancestors. The cultural contacts and environmental surroundings have also played a major role.

This is so true, as Naini herself admits, that at one point she almost gave up at the very beginning of pursuing her independence due to the fear of her family cursing her if she left the man (Tim). Although she had this in mind, she had a strong will and told herself 'Life must continue and whether my family care or not I must establish my own existence!' She just had to hope that someday she would be free, and in the end she became free through a lot of struggles.

Some child marriages do last, as not all men are unkind; however, the workload and childbearing are always the same! Some women are seldom allowed to practise family planning, which was also the case with Naini – she was no exception.

In the olden days, Maasai women had at least a four-year interval before having other children. Although Naini got her children a little over 30 years ago, she was not given the time to do family planning. This was particularly so, especially for ladies living in big towns in order to tie them down. This was also true because the majority of women were housewives.

Such arranged marriages do at times last due to the fact that since the individual concerned does not know a better life than the one she is in, so she is contented with what she has.

There are three ways in which the bridegroom or his family can approach and introduce themselves to the bride's family. Naini's sister Nareyro's engagement followed the third procedure.

The first one is when the mother is still pregnant, the bridegroom-to-be makes a cross sign on the tummy of the expectant mother. That marks the beginning of the relationship between the two families. After doing that, he states these words to the pregnant woman, 'If what you have in your womb is a girl, then I will marry her, and if it is a boy, he will be my great friend.' In the case where a boy is born, the man will then give the newborn baby a heifer, and when he is grown-up he will call him *en-ntauo ai* (my heifer). They will never call one another by name.

The second one is normally the mother of the boy or a lady relative of the boy who approaches the girl and uses a small chain (*e-monyorit*) to tuck onto the beads on the girl's neck, uttering these words, '*Talepo in-kishu a-roi ole Nagida.*'

The girl will object to this, of course, and with annoyance she will tell her mother of the *saoli* (engagement). She will also tell the mother of the warrior that she is only wasting her time because under no circumstances will she ever be married in her home and that the bridegroom is a very ugly man for her to marry.

The third type of engagement which is also practised by the Maa community involves the delivery of cows the very day of circumcision. These are known as *a-enu in-kishu*. When several men are interested in the young bride *e-siankiki* turn up early in the morning each leading *e-nkashe*. All the cows will be tied inside the kraal awaiting the decision of the elders. The family elders will then sit in camera to decide on who to give their daughter to. After deciding, they go and untie all the other calves except the one for the man they want.

This man will be called in and advised to bring a fattened *o-lker o-pir* (ram) the following morning. He will then slaughter the ram for the bride-to-be, who is by then *nenkaibartani*. He will then be told to go back and wait until after recuperation and after the rest of the other ceremonies have been done. During this period, which lasts about nine months, the bride will be in seclusion, being advised by elderly women on how to live as a married woman.

Some days before the final ceremonies of sending off the *e-siankiki*, the bridegroom is ordered to bring some honey for the occasion. In the meantime the bride's family prepares all the ornaments necessary for her decoration on the day of her departure to her new home. This includes preparation of her traditional attire, which has been decorated with beads and freshly oiled, using a ram's fat mixed with *e-reko* (ochre).

On the wedding day – *e-nkolong' e-ishoori/e-elari e-ntito* – the family party of the bridegroom arrives in the afternoon before and sleeps at the bride's home. The following morning the bride and the bridegroom are blessed, using *e-ng'orno naibor* (fresh cream) which is prepared and provided by the mother of the bride that very morning before their departure. The fresh *e-ng'orno naibor* is then put into a horn which will serve as a bowl. It will be dished out to anoint both the bride and the bridegroom, using a reed from a palm tree. This *e-sosian* is used to clean the inside of calabashes with. The bride will carry it later that day to her new home.

The bride and bridegroom are anointed with the fresh cream, *e-ng'orno naibor*, which is applied starting from their foreheads down to their feet. It is used to bless the couple and indicate consent of the parents to give away their daughter. During the send-off just after the blessing, the two will also be instructed on their duties and obligations to one another (*neitanapi*). The girl told, '*Ele payian taa ake kitodua iyiook*', which translated means 'This is the only man we have seen'. She is also told to respect her husband and her in-laws. The man is advised on the same issue. He is told to respect his wife. He is also told that, 'we have given you a stick to use to punish her in case of her shortcomings'. The elders also add, '*Kincoo iyie e-ng'udi amu medami e-nkitok, nemeoshi tol-cata le nkima, amu meari e-nkitok too nkeek naag'ol.*' Literally translated, this means 'A woman is fragile. Don't ever punish her with a log of wood or any other hard object.'

After all this, the girl is warned not to look back during her journey after leaving her parents' home until she reaches her new home because, it is said, once a certain girl looked back when being led and turned into a stone! Such an incident happened at a place called *Eselenkei* and another such stone is at Hells Gate, facing Lake Naivasha, forming one of the gates to climb '*O-loo-nong'ot.*' When translated it means 'it of many valleys' and was probably produced by volcanism in the past.

For the farewell, they are made to pass under *esinandei* held by ceremonial elders at the '*e-nkishomi*'. The bride is escorted by elderly women, a young girl and other family members from the bridegroom's family and *ol-cepulkerra*, who is of the same age group as the groom.

After her departure, the relatives and friends who come to witness the ceremony remain inside the house after the blessing and continue drinking and depart at their own pleasure. Others stay until late in the evening or the following morning.

The bride will be in the middle during the whole trip. She walks very slowly, stopping at any crossway or river. She must not walk over any sticks on the pathway and if she has to, she makes demands for cows, sheep, goats etc. Any obstacles on the path are usually removed by the best man or any other member of the bridal party.

Before leaving her parents' home and during the entire occasion, the bride will have a long string in which she ties knots to keep count of the animals given by her husband and the rest of her in-laws.

On arrival at the bridegroom's home, the bride Nareyro was offered nine cows and a bull by her husband and in the event of a cow leading a calf *En-kiteng narikito o lashe*, it is counted as one, being a bonus to her. Her entitlement of nine cows and a bull excludes heifers, sheep and goats. The bride can also make additional claims such as a cow for drinking that family's milk, a cow for grinding snuff for the husband and a cow for entering the house. Later on, the wife could also reciprocate by giving the husband a cow for accepting her food.

On the evening of her arrival at her new home, she stays with the mother-in-law for three consecutive days and each evening she goes to herd cattle accompanied by her mother-in-law. The purpose of these trips is to enable the young bride to adjust to the new surroundings and to get to know the cows that were given to her and those that belong to her husband, so that she can demand some of the husband's own cows before she will have a sexual relationship with him.

This is done at this stage because in the polygamous Maasai society, men try to outwit the wives so as to reserve the cows for other future wives, so the new bride tries to gain as much as she can. When the husband agrees to give her the cows she has chosen, she will then undress and the man will then break her virginity, and that marks the first time they share the bed. This is so because most of the time, it is the families who arrange the weddings, especially for those youths who are living in the reserve. Sometimes a young man finds himself married without his knowledge if he is living far away from home due to his employment. When he goes back on leave, he finds a wife waiting for him at his parents' *en-kang*.

The second approach to engagement is through the choice of the clan and the family of the man who is going to marry. His mother approaches the chosen girl and cleverly tacks a chain onto her beads. The man's family will then wait to be told of the day when they should return for the hearing of their proposal. During this same trip, the parents usually take tobacco to the girl's parents.

During the second trip, the bridegroom's parents will then take along two elders and one age-mate of the bridegroom as his *ol-cepulkerra*. They also take one heifer and carry a calabash half full of milk, which the would-be *ol-cepulkerra* will take to the bride's family. Customarily the calabash should not be filled to the brim. If filled, it is believed to signify that one is satisfied with everything and does not need to be given the bride for marriage; and does not want to be helped in any way.

On reaching the bride's homestead, the heifer is tied to one pole of the kraal. The visitors go inside the house and join the bride's family. Here the Maasai people do not greet each other as customary. The family of the bride brings a hide and sets it somewhere near the door where the family of the bridegroom will be seated facing the east and are then saluted, *E-ntasupa ilpayiani kituak* (hello, great ones). After the greetings a prayer is said by a chosen elder from the bride's family. The prayer goes like this:

Na-Ai kiomon iyie
Enk-ai incoo iyiook il-tiil omunyak

Kolong' ilepu to loo saen nidoyio to loo ntoluo
– Oh sun rising from the East dawning on the
    west
Enk-ai incoo iyiook il-tiil omunyak
– Give us your lucky rays of blessings
Meishoo iyiook osotua
– Give us peace
Meishoo iyiook ol-ningoo
– Give us understanding
Matejo etejo Enk-ai ayia
Let's say that God has accepted
Metaa anaa ol-donyo le Sirkoik Okaruna
– Let all we beg or pray for, God, be as big as
    the hills of Sirkoik and Karuna.

After every line of prayer that is said by the chosen elder, the rest answer each time in unison like this: *Na-Ai* (God has answered that).

After the prayer, the interview and negotiations are started by the bride's family. The questions and answers are always in parables and usually go like this:

Bride's family	Bridegroom's family
What do you want?	A cow (meaning a girl)
What kind of a cow?	The plain one (also meaning a girl)

If the results are positive, the girl's family will then answer '*Neina kishomi.*' This translates as 'The gate is open for you' and means: 'We have accepted your marriage proposal.'

'How many cattle do you offer as the first sign of dowry?'
Bridegroom: 'Five, a bullock and four heifers!'
In case the family of the bride gives a negative answer by not accepting the marriage proposal, everything brought would be returned back to the groom's family. Such a refusal could only occur if they had received another proposition earlier. In case the family of the proposer refuses to take back

103

what was owed, they are told by the girl's family to wait for the next girl of the same family (in Kimaasai, *nejokini metaanyu siadi*) as a settlement.

The fourth and rarest way of engagement and marriage is when a girl has fallen in love with a man of her own choice and wants to get married to him but is afraid that her parents might object. She usually elopes without her parents' consent.

The fifth one, which is by elopement too, is without the knowledge of both sets of parents, unlike the one above when the parents of the family of the man knows. This is when the family of the bride has refused to marry their daughter to this particular family, because of another proposal, and at times may even involve physical abduction if the girl tries to resist.

The bridegroom will eventually come back for negotiation once again with the in-laws when their tempers have cooled down. Later on the couple will usually send some elders to the girl's family to tell them about this and at the same time to ask them for forgiveness. The bridegroom and the clan elders will go carrying some drinks for compromise. And if the family of the bride agrees, they will then proceed with the marriage process.

First they will go to the bride's home to have their blessings and mandate for their wedding, and the dowry will then be paid, or arrangements made to pay at a later date, then they will live as approved husband and wife thereafter. Most likely they will remain in hiding until the *e-siankiki* is pregnant as this will give them an OK.

This was the case with Naini's mother even though it never materialized for the reasons given earlier about clanism.

In those early days, the belt on the bride's waist was used for record-keeping by tying knots each time she was given a cow or a goat, then the following day after she had been shown and identified each animal, she would then undo the knots. The Maasai people never wrote anything down, but when one cow was missed, the herdsman always noticed when the cows returned to the kraal in the evening. The cows were identified by their horns, colour, or by the tone of its bell, fertility etc.

On any of the three ways of engagement and marriage, the blessings and farewell part are always the same, except in the case of elopement.

In the past, the dowry consisted of only five herds of cattle. At present it depends on what the family wants. Some families prefer to be paid money, unlike olden days. After paying dowry, beer is usually served. The bride, the bridegroom, the best man and the young girl leave after the blessing. These are some Maasai wedding blessings;

Entoropilo	– May you be cleansed
Toiu il-ayiok o i-ntoyie	– May you bear boys and girls
Toisho enol-maati	– May you have many children as that of the grass hopper
Toiki ilarin oo melok	– Beat children in sweet years (years without sickness)
Meishoo i-ntai Enk-Ai i-nkipa	– May God give you slime/ May God give you both organs of sex with their function of reproductive spermatozoon

(This particular prayer was said when Naini was going to her new home – Tim's home.)

The decoration of the bride starts a day before her departure day. On the very morning before she leaves, the bride is dressed up in her ceremonial top garments made of hides (of goat or sheep) and decorated with beads, which are sewn onto the leather in special patterns (*olekesena, ole-kishopo otukusoki too saen*).

During the engagement time, it is important that the families note the clans (*il-gilats*) and the age-group. The Maasai tribal chronological age-group system serves as a guide to the Maasai history and also indicates the past generations to the current one in a narrative form.

Age-group (in Kimassai known as *olporror*, plural *ilporrori*) is observed so that men don't make the mistake of marrying e.g. daughters of their own age group, as to have sexual relations with such girls is considered incestuous. This means all the children of marriages of that particular age group. It also implies therefore that a man can only marry a girl from a higher or lower age group than the one he belongs to himself.

Naini was married to *olporror lo-ilterekeyian or il-kiramat of the emurata e tatene*, meaning the age-group of the right-hand circumcision, but she never underwent all the traditions as such, especially those concerning marriage. Her marriage was never traditionally confirmed, which made it completely different from that of other Maasai girls, including that of her sister Nareyro. It was neither a traditional marriage nor a church marriage. She was not given cows as custom demands, because after the family blessings the day of the marriage, she left with Tim's family in a lorry which was parked just outside her father's home when the blessing was going on.

Besides, she was taken to live in a small town house made of wood and the walls were plastered with soil; in addition, there were no cows. Tim lived there with his mother and his sister-in-law, whose husband was living and working in another town. The idea of asking for the cows never occurred to her, and her mother-in-law did not even intervene on her behalf on the issue.

Usually, in a proper Maasai marriage, on arrival at the bridegroom's home, his family and relatives await the bride (*e-siankiki*) to welcome her to her new home. During the welcome, whenever a woman is brought into the family by way of marriage, it is customary for her husband's relative and their wives to each give an animal to show that they recognize her as a member of the family. The giver and the recipient afterwards call one another after the animal which was given during that occasion.

This occasion is usually meant to help the newly married couple (for the benefit of the bride) to accumulate wealth through gifts, which are usually cows, sheep, goats etc. Naini's sister Nareyro followed this tradition, which is still practised, although now people give cash if requested by the young people or other gifts deemed necessary for city dwellers.

In the olden days, the bridegroom had no right over the cows, goats or sheep given to his bride. In fact he himself was supposed to give her her share of his own cows, which was usually nine head of cattle. He would also give her a cow for performing special duties such as grinding his snuff.

Naini's was an extreme case; had she been living in the traditional family village home, the elders or brothers-in-law could possibly have asked Tim to give her the cows the following morning, as custom demands. Perhaps, had she been living in the village, the village elders could have saved their marriage from breaking up, despite the fact of the many unperformed ceremonies to validate the marriage.

Usually, among the family members, a daughter-in-law during a husband-and-wife dispute calls the elders to a talk and reports the husband if he mistreats her. Naini's case was exceptional. She could even have approached her father-in-law if she thought her treatment was not fair. In this case, Tim could have been asked to pay a fine or slaughtered a cow as compensation for the wounds that she had sustained.

This was never done, despite the many fights that took place during her stay with Tim. Naini's mother-in-law too never took any action on this issue. (In fact, she had always taken sides to support her son. Many times Naini felt that her mother-in-law contributed towards her unhappiness by shouting at her whenever she made minor mistakes, such as going to play with other children within the compound, instead of advising her on what was wrong and what was right. She was still young and didn't see anything wrong in playing. She was just a youth and had no knowledge of how to treat a husband, let alone bring up children. Had she been at the homestead with other ladies, they could have advised her on the day-to-day routine until she actually adopted the new lifestyle and learnt how to bring up children).

These gifts of domestic animals start pouring in the moment the bride sets foot outside her parents' home.

In the past, when a poor person happened to marry a wealthy man's daughter, the girl's father would let his daughter go with some cattle, say 10 or even 20. This was done because the girl's father didn't want his daughter to go and starve.

After all this, the bride will keep demanding from her new family members. For example, she will not sit down at her new home until she has been given a gift, and these demands will continue till late evening. The following morning, she will now be shown her own cattle by her husband. From there on, she is now at liberty to do whatever she desires but in consultation with her mother-in-law until the three days are over, but cannot make any more demands except on the night of meeting her husband finally.

As for the girl's family after all the ceremonies have been performed, that is, engagement, circumcision and marriage, they are ready to let their daughter go away, but before that, there are decoration to be done.

After the final ceremony, the young maiden (*e-siankiki*) is decorated by the older women. A copper wire is fixed around her upper arm, at the same time they also fix one on *e-ntakule* (lower arm). On the young lady's lower part of the leg, on the right leg (*e-nkeju e tatene*) they will put *enk-alulung'a*. Then on both her legs they fix copper wires around the ankles, or only on the right ankle if she wishes.

All these things are done before she leaves her parents' home. All the ornaments offered by her family are prepared during the period she is *enkaibartani*. She will always use them during special occasions as not all of them are useable in day-to-day life.

As customary, after the final ceremony to be released from seclusion (*abolu e-nkaibartani*), the *e-monyorit*, which was her engagement chain or rather ring, would then be transferred and attached to *i-nkonito oo i-nkiyiaa*, the long leather earflaps of the right ear lobe. She will then keep this chain until the time she will be circumcising her own children, and the chain will always serve as a wedding ring.

During the same occasion, she will then add scrolled earrings, known in Kimaasai as *isurrutia*, which are made of copper, along with *isulan*, which have the same design but smaller, and black and white beads (*ilmoru*).

Marriage usually takes place after circumcision graduation, except in cases such as Naini's – she was allowed to go back to school afterwards. So is the payment of dowry which will be paid in instalments. Rarely do the Maasai people call their relatives by name, customarily it is based on what is given.

As for the names used for the girl's family members, the son-in-law will call the girl's mother *e-nkaputani ai* and the girl's father *ol-aputani lai*, or *entau ai* if he had given him a heifer. The bridegroom will call the sister-in-law *parsintant*.

If a Maasai man has many wives, he builds himself and his age-mates a special house known as *osingira* which is outside the ceremonial house. The man will then stay there and only goes to visit the wives in turns. He also eats his meals there and has private meetings there.

Before the man brings in another wife, he ascertains that his first wife, who will officiate in the ceremony, has been properly married and all the bride price has been delivered to her parents' home in full. This includes four heifers and one bull or bullock, all of which must be of the same colour, with no scars and no unusual peculiarities, two female sheep and one fattened ram which is slaughtered and the fat used for mixing the ochre for the make-up smeared on the bodies the day of the ceremony. Some of the fat is also mixed with meat to make a special dish known as *ol purda*, which is then put into a container (*olnoos*) which the bride carries along with her on her back to her new home.

Although Naini didn't undergo the above formalities she can relate other cases in her home area, e.g. that of her sister Nareyro.

The bridegroom also brings a lamb, which he gives to the mother-in-law, and afterwards he calls her *paker*, which means the one to whom I gave a lamb. In Maasai tradition, the son-in-law cannot call her by her name but rather refers to her as mother (*Yeyio*) or *paker/e-nkaptani ai.*

The bride also gives a heifer to her father-in-law, and often he offers her one too on arrival, so that thereafter they call each other *paashe.* A brass ornament is also given to the *e-nka-putani* by the bridegroom as a sign of marrying her daughter and this symbolizes respect to her. As for the newly wed lady, an ornament is put on her right ear-lobe and another on the right leg (*olmukurit*).

Seldom will a Maasai family remain childless owing to the fact that the man is impotent. The spirit of comradeship and communialism that was bred and nurtured during the period of moranship is carried on into married life. In the case of a first wife being barren, she will encourage the husband to marry a younger girl to bear children with him. In this case she will not be divorced, she will remain within the family. Thus the co-wife may both in theory and practice give a child to the first wife. This is done at child-birth, as was the case with Naini's sister.

This action will build up their relationship. This is done so that the child can inherit what the barren woman owns and also give her protection and keep her company. The property will then remain within the family.

This was the case with Naini's sister Nareyro and Naimutie. Soon after birth, she gave Naimutie the baby. By giving the other woman a child at birth (*aishooyo e-nkerai tol-togom*), this means that the child will be breastfed by the adoptive mother Naimutie and not the biological mother Nareyro. When the baby is born and the mother (adoptive mother) is without milk due to the body chemistry as in this case, or cannot breastfeed due to other reasons, the baby is then given milk mixed with some medicinal juices boiled from stripped barks of trees or roots (*ol-mairo*) to dilute it, known in Kimaasai as *e-nkare pus* – greyish water. Never should a Maasai baby be given undiluted milk as this can bring about stomach troubles to the newborn. While this is still going on, in the meantime, she will go on breastfeeding until the milk at birth has been induced and she has enough milk (in Kimaasai *aitanak-enkerai o-meiturupaki ilki*).

It is not adoption as such, but a formality which is witnessed and confirmed by members of the clan. In principal, it is more of an understanding within the family.

At her old age, if she never bore any son, and the child she was given is a girl, then she is permitted by society to retain the lone daughter at home. She will not get married. She will stay, and after circumsision, she is permitted to bear children at home who will later inherit their grandparents' wealth. This is done so that the wealth remains within the family after her death. A sister, too, may give her sister a child. This matter is usually kept secret, not letting the child know, and it will always remain as a family affair.

On such occasions, a sacrifice is usually performed for the childless mothers. A spotless goat is usually slaughtered (in Kimaasai *ol-kine o-sinya*). Alternatively a plant is used for the blessing ceremony. The leaves are dipped into the calabash full of native beer, then into a second calabash full of a mixture of milk and water (*i-naishi o kule*).

This is what the diviner (*oloiboni*) uses for blessings after the sacrifice. He begins with the sacrifice and slits through its neck, which is held out towards him as fast as possible, and most of the blood is collected in a calabash to be used later for preparing *monono*. As the animal lies kicking, he blesses it, then the rest of the ceremony is performed by his assistant, who finishes skinning the animal. Later, he says some prayers and blessings, stuffs grass and leaves into the mouth of a calabash so that the liquid comes out in droplets. After that, he rubs his hands together to dry them.

During this occasion, some prayers are said and special songs sung by women, such as '*e-nkai kiomon iyie entomono*', meaning 'Lord we beseech you to give us children'.

After the adoption ceremony, the co-wife, after this prayer, gives the mother of the child a heifer for their greater understanding and they will thereafter call one another *paa a-she* after the cow which was given.

Usually after this transaction, which is carried out within the family members, just before the end of the ceremony, the

111

ritual expert known as *oloiboni* will usually cut a piece of the goat's skin for a ring (*olkereti*) for the blessed mother, which he will put on the middle finger. He will also wash the blessed mother with the mixture of boiled herbs by the junction of a footpath while saying these words in Kimaasai, '*Kitudung'o o-enet tenaa oltung'ani apa likiteena – nikitalaa iyie. Naa tenaa E-nkai apa nikiteena nikitoomono mikinchoo e-ishoi.*' This prayer translates as follows: We break the fetters that bind you. If it is a man who has tied you, but if it is God who has bound you (who refused to grant you offspring), we will entreat Him on your behalf.

There are other ceremonies performed by the *oloiboni*, who combines the qualities of spiritual leader, ritual expert and healer and also performs other blessings for the barren at *emanyatta olamal loo nkituak* such as a special blessings ceremony carried out for women to be fruitful and obtain offspring, which is more or less the same as the one discussed above. During this particular blessing the parents and the elders sip the native beer then spit it onto their chests and onto the ground to appease the spirits. Such ceremonies are usually preceded by a slaughter and meat-eating, and drinking of *enaisho olchani*, which is brewed by mixing honey and *isuguro*, the seeds of the sausage tree after they have been dried. It is brewed in a hide bag.

Other blessings are from older people. When Naini was blessed by her grandmother (*kokoo*), she was told this: 'Listen, my granddaughter, my time to depart is drawing nearer as I will soon be going to sleep for good. Before that time comes, come closer by me because I want to bless you, my beloved Naini.' She then asked Naini to open both her palms and then she spat onto them, then after that she instructed Naini to rub the spittle on her feet while she said these words in Kimaasai: '*Toropilo, tumunyana, mikinchoo E-nkai enkishon nayengieng'unye.*' (Literal translation: Be cleansed, be lucky, may God give you life that generates slowly.' While she was saying these words of blessings, Naini was only left to answer each time at the end of every word like this, '*Na-Ai*', which means, if God wishes.

Naini's grandmother didn't live much longer after that blessing. It seems that older people could foretell their own destiny. To her grandmother, life didn't have any meaning any more. She was very, very old when she departed. Naini used to wash her just like a small baby.

In those early Maasai marriages, the parents played a great role in identifying the girl they would wish their son to marry. Without his knowledge, they would secretly study the ladies to know their habits and character, and the history of their family line and background. The girl's parents too would do the same to ensure that the custody of their daughter was in good hands. This is the case in a traditional and customary marriage. The tradition may extend to the point of marrying a 12-year-old girl to a man of 50 years, so long as she is not of the same clan and not fathered by the same age-set and so long as the bridegroom's family fits the above conditions. The girl has no say. Usually, before marrying a second wife, he must clear what was outstanding as dowry for the first wife and must undergo all the traditional ceremonies as discussed earlier.

The idea of divorce was a remote concept in the older generation as somehow the Maasai women fully accepted the polygamous way of life. Naini once asked one Maasai lady, her friend Nyamalo, why is it that Maasai women accept all these things, especially polygamy? In response, she said, 'It is better the devil you know than the one you don't know!' When pressed further on the same issue, she told her that when your husband doesn't turn up, then you know at least where to find him in case of emergency. When he slaughtered a goat or a sheep for her, in the olden days, the cow-wife would get a share of the meat, Nyamalo went on to explain, unlike now, when some men take everything to the girlfriend, abandoning the first wife. Naini herself does not approve of polygamous marriages but these things happen quite often.

Maasai customary marriages are recognized in Kenya

only if the man has met all the conditions and requirements and has fully performed all the ceremonies to complete the marriage according to the Maasai traditions. The last rituals and downpayment (dowry) consists of four heifers and one bull, one sheep to the mother of the girl, and a heifer to the father etc. The same applies when marrying another wife. The dowry can thus be given at once or in parts depending on the assets of the bridegroom. Usually the family of the girl takes into consideration this point to avoid any further suffering of the newly wed couple in the future. Taking into account that most of the Maasai are dependent on their cattle, it would not be wise to let the man give away all his cows if he is not rich as this will make him poorer! This means that the girl can still be married despite the fact that the total dowry has not been given, in order to enable the couple to start a new life without any constraint. The man can gradually give what he owes to the girl's parents within the agreed period. When the time elapses before he has cleared his dowry, then he will get a reminder. This means they will send someone to remind him. However, if the husband is still not able to give the dowry, the sons will have to honour that before they are allowed to perform certain rituals, such as marriage and circumcision of their children.

9

THE PAINS OF MOTHERHOOD

The day when Naini started to have pains in her lower abdomen and back, many times she felt the urgent need to go to the toilet, but as she sat in a frog-like position there was nothing coming out, just a little urine.

Since the toilet was a pit latrine, she thought the child might drop and fall into the pit and die. For this reason, she told her mother-in-law who in turn assured her that the child was still a long way off.

Naini still doubted this, so, instead of going each time to the same toilet, she just went behind the nearby bushes and hid herself to urinate there. She imagined that, if the unborn infant fell in the pit latrine, he or she would be eaten by *ilkuru* (maggots). She imagined that it would die quickly because they would bite it and enter into the ears, the nose and finally through the mouth. She imagined that while this was happening, others would be eating the flesh, including the eyes!

It was just after the short rains in November, so the pit latrine was nearly full to the brim and there were layers of maggots, each one of them struggling for survival of the fittest climbing over one another not to sink and to reach the surface for fresh air and to be able to eat the fresh excrement Naini was just dropping above the yellowish liquids of human faeces, urine and rainwater. The fact that she had to part her legs to be able to aim at the hole in the middle of the wooden bars even added to her fears. Her bottom was hanging in the air parallel to her feet and so was her protruding belly due to too much expansion – nearly touching the wooden floor separating her and the maggots.

In the village where Naini came from, in those days most people did not use the pit latrine because during the rainy season it harboured mosquitoes, which in turn brought malaria. Apart from that danger, during the rainy season the temporary walls were swept away, occasioning far worse dangers for both human and livestock. So to minimize these dangers they just went to the forest to manure it.

In addition to the mountain of problems Naini had experienced just after her marriage, the second day she was in labour, her so-called husband was nowhere to be found. He was not at the family home! She did not know what to expect at such a time. She started to wonder what she would do if the baby arrived, when there was nobody to assist her. She did not know the exact symptoms even though she recalled once hearing her mother say that usually the pains start at the lower part of the abdomen and then the back aches. She had no idea how long the pains would last, unlike her children now, who know exactly what to expect through reading books and even watching film shows on such issues. She informed her mother-in-law that she felt ill and unable to work that day so she would not carry on the usual duties of making tea (*shaai*) for the teacher and her children.

Naanyu was not pleased to hear this as she knew that Naini was now going to have a baby and she would have to undertake all the housework. She yelled at her, saying that she was just complaining for nothing so as to sleep instead of preparing breakfast for the children! Can you imagine, Naini not yet 14 years of age and made to work for them even at the point of giving birth! All the same, Naini repeatedly told her that she felt ill and unable to work, no matter what she would do to her. She got the message all right, realizing that there was a genuine problem and a serious one. Hence she went to look for a car to take Naini to the hospital.

The hospital was situated at Kericho, which was about 60 to 80 miles away. On arrival, Naini was immediately taken to the maternity ward. In the labour ward. Women were wailing due to pains, speaking in different languages. Naini at this point cried and she remembers saying, '*Oi Yeyioo ai!*' A woman whose bed was next to hers and who the nurses were urging her to continue pushing, was wailing at the top of her voice. The poor woman had a lot of difficulties as the child was nowhere near to be born and it was only water which was flowing.

The water went across the room under several beds, including Naini's and when she finally delivered, the child was abnormal. After a long struggle the baby only cried once then it died. The nurses were running up and down in the ward because the woman had developed other problems from the shock of what she got. On seeing this, Naini became even more terrified than ever before. She wondered if she was also going to be beset by the same misfortunes and she had laboured for over eight hours. She had never attended any clinic during her pregnancy and neither was she assigned a midwife as all the other young mothers. Her mother-in-law did not really care for her. She had tried to bear it alone, having no one to tell. Her husband Tim was not there to help her at this critical moment. But she was lucky at least his mother took her to hospital because both of them would have died as she could not have a normal delivery.

The nurse took her to a changing room then she commanded her to remove everything including her underwear. As Naini tried to untie the string of her knickers, her hands were trembly, shaking so much that she was incapable of untying it! The kind nurse, on seeing this, quickly stepped forward to her aid. And this was not all, she also helped her to tie the hospital outfit, which was some sort of an apron worn especially as a covering for the chest and abdomen, knee-length, with four strings at the back, using the Girl Guide style of knot. After this, she escorted her to a bed which was going to be hers for the rest of the week. She told her to lie down so that she could be examined by a doctor. She then put a curtain around her bed so that the rest of the people in the room could not see what they were doing.

Soon a white doctor (European) appeared, accompanied

by the same nurse. This was the first time Naini had been attended to by a white doctor. The doctor spoke English and the nurse in turn explained to Naini, in Kiswahili this time. The pains had subsided in both her stomach and her back, perhaps because of fear or because it was time for the unborn baby to rest. He then told Naini to lie on her back. After that he placed an instrument on her stomach then bent over to listen to the child's heartbeats. After examining her, he then briefed the nurse on her condition. The doctor then put on gloves and inserted two fingers to feel the head of the unborn child, while touching Naini's stomach with the left hand. During the examination, the doctor decided to speak in English once again to the nurse, who in turn spoke to Naini in Kiswahili. '*Mama uchungu ulianza lini?*' 'Mama, when did the pains start?'

Naini said in Kiswahili '*jana*', meaning yesterday. Before the arrival of the doctor, the nurse had shaved all her pubic hair.

The nurse then assured her that the doctor had said the baby was in position so that she shouldn't worry but to try to relax. As if she had just found her tongue, Naini told them that she felt like going for a short call. The doctor wrote something, then left.

The nurse drew the curtains sideways then directed Naini to a WC which was within the ward and which was just a few yards away from where she was lying. On opening the toilet door, to her surprise, it was a different kind of toilet altogether, unlike the ones she had used in the past. It was not the same as the one they used when they went to Nairobi during the Music Festival at the hotel, which had a raised bowl-shaped fixture and flushed with water. This particular one had no smell, nor the maggots. Naini was told later by the same nurse that it was the Indian sort of toilet – a wide white basin dug in and cemented as part of the toilet floor. The floating water in it was very clean after it has been flushed. After all these observations, Naini closed the door behind her, then lifted the apron she was wearing and sat down half kneeling to be able to urinate, but away

from the main basin, afraid of what might happen.
It was once again the same feeling. She had very little urine as she had not eaten anything that morning at home, neither had she eaten the night before. After this, she stood upright and let the apron roll downwards as before, then opened the toilet door. On opening the door, the nurse was standing by the door and started asking Naini why she had taken so long in the toilet. Before Naini could open her mouth, she asked her why she hadn't flushed the water. In addition, she asked, 'Why didn't you urinate directly in the basin? Mama, why did you do like this?'

Naini told her of her fear in case the child fell into the toilet and the consequences that might follow. The nurse then laughed, took her hand and said 'Let's go to your bed.' At her bedside, she went on to explain to Naini that the child doesn't just drop. She then confirmed that the doctor had said if by 4.00 p.m. Naini hadn't delivered, he would give her some injection to induce more labour pains because the child seemed a little tired.

'Your brother-in-law has already signed the letter of consent in case it warranted a Caesarean operation,' she concluded. When she was telling Nani this, her mother-in-law and her brother-in-law had already left the hospital in fear of driving back in the dark because the roads leading home were untarmacked and too muddy.

Naini covered her head and cried silently because she was now on her own, so far away from home, had no friends to comfort her and wondered what would happen next.

What will happen if they fail to return to come and fetch me and the child, she thought. Who will pay for my hospital bills and where would I get money to even board a bus to take me nearer to my homeland?

By the end of that afternoon, the same nurse, accompanied by a male nurse, came towards her bed, pushing another bed with wheels. She was then transferred to it and taken to the labour ward, which was attached to the main maternity ward. In there, there were several nurses and two doctors. Before taking Naini to that room, they had injected her to induce labour pains (*a-saisai*), so she was now suffering and undergoing the pains of childbirth. Every part of her body was hurting and she was sweating a lot. They were holding her down because she was screaming. a nurse standing by her head was wiping her face with a wet towel, while urging her to push. Naini felt like vomiting but nothing was coming out. Her legs were held apart. The very nurse who was wiping her face told her to breathe in and now push. She repeated it again and again but nothing happened.

On realizing this, the doctor told them it was impossible. They had to use forceps. Despite the pains, Naini overhead him saying this. He went on further to demand to be brought other equipment. 'I have to cut her a bit to expand the outlet, then I can use the forceps to pull the child, otherwise she will not deliver,' he concluded.

The moment Naini heard him say this, she screamed even louder – before he even cut her.

He said to her, 'I am sorry, madam, but we have to do it this way to save you and the child.'

By then she was completely held to the bed by the male nurses so she had no chance of escaping the operation as she couldn't run away.

'Now push,' they said, again and again, until Naini finally delivered after a long struggle. The doctor then announced that it was a baby boy. Before this announcement, just after delivery, he had held both feet of her newborn baby upwards, head facing downwards, and hit gently on the baby's back. That was when the child started to cry and not before, and at the same time passed urine! Before showing Naini the baby, he had already cut the umbilical cord – she just had a glance of it. Before taking it away to the nursery, they made sure that they had put a label for identification around the tiny wrist of Naini's baby. Soon after that the female nurse disappeared with it. Despite the pains she was now going through being stitched, Naini was somehow relieved to learn that they were both safe and in good health.

The bedding was changed. After that, Naini was transferred to her original bed. She began thinking of what had taken place during the past few hours and what to expect after this, but before long, she was fast asleep.

At around 10.00 p.m. that night, she was woken up by a nurse to drink some tea. She was still feeling very tired, to the extent of not being able to drink the cup of tea. Due to the struggle during delivery, all her muscles were strained, so she just thanked the nurse for it then went back once again to sleep. She had forgotten all about the baby!

Very early the following morning, Naini thought it was about 6.00 a.m. but had no wristwatch, she was awakened by a nurse pushing the administrative medicine supply trolley for the patients. She gave Naini two tablets and water in a small plastic cup and waited for her to take the dose, and then took away the plastic cup. After that Naini went back to sleep, although not for long as she was once again awakened to go and take a shower. She came off the bed slowly, taking care not to fall, as she was nearly unable to walk or even stand up because of the many stitches she had. The kind nurse rushed to her aid otherwise she could have fallen down. She helped her back into bed, then went away and returned carrying a bedpan and helped her sit on it, after drawing the curtains around her bed to shut off the other patients from seeing what was happening. This was a shallow pan used as a toilet by a person confined to bed. This went on for two days. Naini was a bit distressed to find herself in the situation of being incapable of standing up on her own to go to the toilet. She was also embarrassed because it was as if she was urinating in bed.

The worst was yet to be experienced. As she painfully tried to sit up, with a lot of strain in order to pass urine, the urine burnt the lips of her private parts where she had been cut the night before. This incident reminded Naini of the pain she went through the first few days after circumcision. She was even more embarrassed when the nurse started giving her a towel bath in bed.

At last it was time to rest, she thought, but no sooner did the nurse return carrying the baby for breastfeeding. As she tried to breastfeed, her nipples hurt so much that she was

121

nearly in tears. When she looked at them, they had cracked. She thought the baby was sucking the life out of her, as if it was drinking blood! She thought of Kitasioyia's story when she crawled out of bed to eat the meat, and was frightened by the thought.

But as the days passed by, Naini got used to the baby and forced herself to eat and drink the tea which was supplied by the hospital in order to be able to have enough milk to breastfeed. But the first two days she had nightmares.

The following day, the family returned to visit her at the hospital. Naini's mother-in-law was very, very happy that she was once again a grandmother. They brought her some millet porridge in a tea flask, which they took away with them by the end of each visit.

The one week at the hospital passed very quickly. Soon it was time to leave for home and start once again the day-to-day housework as before.

During her one-week stay at the hospital, day in, night out, women were always wailing due to various types of pains. There were those who wailed due to anguish after losing a child or a relative at childbirth or after an operation. There were those who were wailing due to natural pains such as labour pains during delivery and before delivery, while others, including Naini, were wailing due to discomfort after birth. As an example, on the second day after delivery, as Naini tried with difficulty to sit up properly, it was nearly impossible, so she laid the baby by her side and moved closer to it to be able to breastfeed it.

One woman whose bed was to her left, swore never to sleep with her husband again! Whether she kept her word, God knows, but Naini doubted it because a day after she delivered, they were happily talking and laughing together.

That night, before Naini went to sleep, the sister in charge notified her that she would be discharged in the morning. Naini's old worries returned. Naini then asked herself a question: was her situation going to change now that she had delivered, or was it going to worsen? That night, her mind pondered many problems until at last she went to sleep.

Next morning she woke up as usual, took her shower then went back to her bed and waited for the nurse to take her temperature and give her the usual morning tablets. Then she had her breakfast. After that she breastfed the baby then returned it to the nursery.

Just a little after 8.30 a.m., Naini's brother-in-law arrived in the ward. She told him that she was going to be discharged that day. He then handed the baby's clothes – a nappy, a sweater, a vest and, to crown it, a large bath towel to wrap around the baby. The sister in charge and the doctor arrived. The nurse, who was going to leave after the night shift, told her brother-in-law to leave the ward and wait in the waiting room. After the usual rounds, the doctor prescribed some medication for Naini to take home with her.

After that the nurse returned, accompanied by Naini's mother-in-law and brother-in-law. Her brother-in-law left them, to go and settle the hospital bills and to buy the medicine the doctor had just prescribed.

Meanwhile, the nurse was helping her to dress the baby. Naini put on her simple maternity dress because her brother-in-law hadn't brought a dress for her – he had thought that his mother had catered for that. He was annoyed by this fact but he tried not to show it; by nature he was always very kind to others.

After this, they all left the hospital ward. Naini said good-bye to some ladies who had been in the same ward during her stay. They then boarded the pick-up and drove all the long way more or less in silence, except when the baby cried her mother-in-law told her to breastfeed it and how to hold it properly.

The family slaughtered a sheep so that she could drink fat and some herbal bone soup. It was not pleasant to drink the fat (*aok eilata*) but one was usually forced to! It made her feel very weak and she had diarrhoea due to it. Throughout this period she was unable to eat anything else. All these were considered normal. After delivery the child's head was not round, and she recalls seeing her mother-in-law massaging the child's head to shape it. She would sit for hours by the fire

123

place warming her hands then proceed to massage the baby's body, using some oil.

After only a few days of rest she embarked on the house-work just as before, but this time, with a child on her back as she had no one to assist her nursing the baby.

When her first child was approaching one year, the second baby was due, as spacing children was never observed by Tim. Tim and Naini lived in two worlds, trying to follow the tradition and at the same time trying to follow the European lifestyle, and fell in between as neither fitted in since they were living in town. This time round she also nearly lost her life as a result of inadequate blood caused by lack of spacing of children, hard work and excessive fatigue. Her stay at hospital was a relief for her, availing time for enough rest. On arriving home, she had only a few days to stay with her child before she resumed on the usual household chores.

It was not long before her fourth pregnancy as she was not allowed to do family planning. At the age of 17 she had four young children to take care of. She cried whenever the children cried. Her situation was difficult and exceedingly challenging; being an inexperienced mother was coupled with mistreatment from the family. She was a child herself and needing parental guidance and love, but with none of these forthcoming, she had to learn to give her love to her children. Many a time, she ran away to her stepfather's home to report mistreatment from her husband, but that did not solve the problem – in Maasai *alo kitala*, which means sanctuary for a runaway wife. Traditionally, whenever there is a misunderstanding between a married couple, the complainant will call for a meeting with the elders to discuss and find out who is at fault. Each time, Naini was forced to go back to her so-called husband. The man was always the winner in such matters, or rather the rules always favoured the man and not his wife!

As the years went by, Naini strove to find a permanent consolation for her destroyed childhood and a way out of the unending sufferings, but to no avail until much later after their separation. She was determined to update her education, and to develop a profession . It proved very difficult at the beginning but she would endure through thick and thin. The scarcity of funds made it even harder.

From all the beatings and mistreatment by her husband. Naini developed a lot of resentment towards men. They felt more superior to women and had a negative attitude toward them. She wanted to run away, go very far away, but had nowhere to run to and also no courage to abandon her young ones. She knew that leaving her children would be abandoning her responsibilities as a mother. This should never happen! Naini's mother-in-law contributed enormously to her miseries. She was cruel and inconsiderate. She added an extra workload on her to care for another woman's children while she went to teach, without paying her a salary, instead of employing her own maid. The lady in question was Tim's distant relative, who was favoured by the mother-in-law because she was earning and she looked down on the little uneducated Naini, whom they decided to mistreat. How cruel of them to take advantage of her!

At times, Naini had to carry one child on her back and another in her arms, placing it on her protruding belly. What a life it was then!

Now it is not the same. Naini sits back and smiles and admires what her children are from the hard work she did in the past, proud to have never abandoned them.

Naini got very depressed over having been denied her education, and most of all for the suffering she underwent from Tim. It was so hard at times that she had to go to other people's houses begging for food to feed her kids. The man at times went for weeks without leaving her any money. He would disappear as soon as he was paid his salary, depriving Naini of any income for her own maintenance.

It was on one late night that the man returned home after squandering all of his money that he almost finished her off. It all started when Naini asked him what had happened and why he had left her and the children for so many days without food. He picked a quarrel because he didn't want her to ask him anything. When Naini started to explain to him that they had been without food for several days, forcing her to go to the neighbours to beg for food, he started to beat her up. In vain she went on to inform him that the landlord had been to the house and taken some household items to sell to be able to recover his rent. He didn't listen. He went on beating her. The following day the man explained to the landlord that he had been fired by his employer and it was due to this that he was unable to pay the rent, and that he was going to raise the money in a few days.

After this incident Naini decided enough was enough and that she had to find a solution to her endless problems. She thought of what would become of her if she did not find a job soon. She was determined to do something and vowed not to just sit back and watch her destruction. The following day she decided to go in search of a job and was lucky, after some weeks of struggle, to find a part-time job as an artist with the Voice of Kenya. It was not a well-paying job, but a humble start to a career, which was much better than having nothing at all. Considering that she didn't have any experience, she accepted the job in order to be able to support her young ones.

It was due to all these hardships that Naini decided to work even harder and swore to herself that she would not let herself go. She had to keep her head above the water. There was no way she was just going to sit idle and do nothing. Instead of resorting to self-pity, she thought of her children, whose lives, future and well-being depended solely on her, otherwise they would perish or later suffer the same consequences of forced marriage from their cruel father. The only solution to this was to keep the children with her. But how? Without any income it would be impossible! She resolved to work hard to obtain some financial resources which would enable her to protect her young ones from their cruel father and bring them up in a calm environment. But she had to maintain cool if she was to tackle what was ahead of her and realize her goal successfully.

Naini's mind drifted back to the past, focusing on her homestead, her friends, her wasted education and the present situation she was in. She was astonished by the fast pace of life and most of all the many changes that had taken place in so short a time. She thought of the mountainous problems she had gone through. While she was still in the midst of weighing her ordeals and plans at hand, the landlord walked in and started once again removing some of the items from the house. When she asked him what was happening, the landlord explained that it was due to nonpayment of rent. To her disbelief, Naini nearly fainted as she did not know where she would go with the children if she was evicted from the rented house. Noticing her helpless and dismay, the landlord told her that he was going to keep them until Tim paid the rent in full. He, however, cautioned that if Tim failed to pay, he would have no choice but to sell them so as to recover his money.

Naini dreaded to think of his next move after all this. It was obvious once there was nothing to sell to recover the rents, the landlord would kick them out of the house! Where was she going to go with the children? She tried to reassure herself not to worry but to let things take their natural course as worrying would serve no useful purpose.

Two more days and nights had passed and still there was no sign of the man. How was she going to solve these problems if the man did not turn up in the next few days?

It was during his absence that Naini finally made her decision. She would go and take up the job offered as an artist irrespective of whether the man objected. Nothing mattered now, because she was not going to sit down and watch her children starve of hunger just because the man was going to beat her. After all, he had been mistreating her all along for no cause; this time she was ready to suffer with a cause.

She left the house early the next morning and went to the Voice of Kenya. She requested to see the Controller of the Vernacular Services. She was allowed to see him and she explained her problems, giving the reasons why she had not turned up earlier. She was interviewed again and told to come back the following day for the results.

The following day she was informed she could undertake a

part-time job as an artist if she accepted the terms. She immediately agreed, after being given the terms and conditions of the contract. The Controller then went on to tell her she would work for one women's programme once a week and one children's programme also once a week, transmitted every Wednesday and every Saturday. The pay respectively was going to be 40 shillings per programme of 15 minutes, totalling 80 shillings per week! Her heart was filled with joy after hearing the good news. It was not much, but a good beginning to being exposed and getting a chance to gain some experience. That was how her struggle started.

After some days the man returned, and when Naini explained to him that the landlord had taken some of the household properties, once again he was not amused.

As usual he started the endless strifes and quarrels which always resulted in a fight! It was such a ferocious fight that it ended up with casualties. Naini had to go to hospital. He had thrown a bottle, aiming at her face, and Naini had fortunately managed to dodge it hitting her forehead, but it hit her hand. Blood gushed from the deep cut inflicted on her hand. There were bloodstains all over the house, up to the ceiling of the two-roomed house they were living in.

At that time her brother Leshoo had come from Narok at the beginning of the week to visit them in Nairobi, at a place called Westlands, during his school holidays. He had intended to stay with them for one month as he was still going to school. He was then in standard four. Her grief-stricken younger brother took a baby's napkin to tie around her arm to stop the bleeding. They were both crying terribly from the violent outburst. They fled the house, leaving the man and the children, who were fast asleep by that time. That night, they managed to go to the hospital through the help of a Samaritan whom they had stopped to ask for a lift as they had no money to hire a taxi. They had then remained at the hospital till morning as they were afraid to return to the house, which was a long walk in the dark night and with the fatigue after losing a lot of blood.

The following day, the man drove off with the children.

Naini and her brother remained behind as they had no money for their bus fare. The departure of Tim, the children and the closure of their house by the landlord became a big problem for Naini and her brother Leshoo. They were now without shelter, had no food and could not think of what to do next. Naini was now very worried and uncertain of her future. She had to think fast otherwise they could fall into more serious troubles if they had to stay outside in the cold with their few belongings. They could be attacked by thieves. The police might also get attracted by their condition and might want to arrest them and, worst of all, they had no money with them even to pay a fine. Their condition might warrant their deportation to the countryside, and this was the last thing Naini would let happen, especially now when she was waiting to start her part-time job with the VOK. She adamantly said no to anything that would deprive her of the opportunity to start her new job.

Naini was still contemplating all this when her brother suddenly interrupted her thoughts, 'Look, Naini; there is the landlord on his way back from his office.' She hoped the landlord might know where her children were, because on their return to the house that morning, it was a shock to them to find out that the children were missing and the house locked. On enquiring from the neighbours they were made to understand that the man drove off with the children that very morning but they had no idea where he was heading.

The landlord informed her that Tim had told him that he was heading to his home in Maasai land. The landlord felt sorry for them, and especially for Naini, whose condition looked pathetic; her clothes were covered with bloodstains from the beating of the previous night, she had a plastered hand and was looking very worried, tired and hungry. The landlord then offered them a meal at his home, which was just near the former house rented by Tim.

While the food was being cooked by his wife, he let Naini have a shower and change into clean clothes from the lot that Tim had left there. He also offered them accommodation for that night to allow Naini time to settle down a bit while she was still trying to sort out what to do next. This was not going to be easy; one night was not enough to find a solution. She was in a difficult situation, made worse by the fact that she had not a single penny with her to facilitate any movement within the town or to buy their food, let alone accommodation! What was she to do, she wondered? The accommodation offered by Mr Shah was only for the night, but all in all they were very grateful for the hospitality and kindness from the landlord's family.

Naini asked their host if he needed any helper in his office or a house servant, but unfortunately Mr Shah told her he already had more than enough workers. She thought to herself, perhaps he had enough as he claimed, but maybe it was due to her condition that he saw that she would not be able to work with a plastered hand.

That night while in bed, Naini cried bitterly. She couldn't close her eyes. She was helplessly thinking of what to do the following day. She thought of her children, of her brother and of herself and wondered what the future had in store for them until at last she fell asleep.

The following day, after breakfast, Mr Shah gave them some money to start them off and wished them good luck. Naini was very grateful for what he did for them and promised to repay the money some day. Mr Shah in turn cheered her up and said it was his pleasure. He went on to say that he understood what she was going through and he praised her for being such a brave young lady and asked her to keep it up – patience paid.

She in turn thanked Mr Shah once again and informed him that in a week's time, she would start a part-time job with the Broadcasting Corporation. She went on to share with him her sadness at having been rendered handicapped. How would she prepare her script?

Mr Shah came up with a bright idea. He simply said that she could ask a friend to write it down while she dictated it! He bid them goodbye.

Accompanied by her brother, and using part of the money

they were given by Mr Shah, she took a bus to South B, where she knew a gentleman who was her adoptiver-father's age-mate. She explained to him all her problems and difficulty of finding accommodation and requested him to assist them for some time while she sought an alternative and also until she started working so that she would be able to pay her rent.

Naini and her brother prepared the script and at the end of the week she went to record her programmes for the first time. The following week she was paid her dues. From her first income, she could now afford to pay bus fares for her brother Leshoo to go back home and inform her foster-father of what had happened. She also asked him to tell him that she had made up her mind never to return to Tim's home. She would rather die than continue living in such con-ditions. She wrote a letter to that effect, explaining the whole situation to them. She realized that she was lucky to have grown up in that family, for apart from the mistreatment of being forced to marriage at an early age, she at least had had a chance to enter a classroom even though not for many years. There were, and still are, children who had all the facil-ities and the freedom to study, but never took that oppor-tunity seriously.

Naini now says, perhaps if she had had everything, if her real father had offered her all the comforts she would have been reluctant to work so hard. But she doubts it. What would have been the case if she had had all that she required in her life? It's all unimaginable. On the other hand, she appreciates that it was after all for the better as things were, because this moulded her into a more solid person and gave her the courage to face and handle many difficult situations of life as they came. She dreads to imagine what would have become of her if she had never gone to school at all! No doubt she would by now be an old woman worn out by hard-ships, childbearing and the workload in the countryside. I suppose, she says, when one has nothing better against which to compare the past or to what is at hand, then it doesn't hurt so much. But when you know something better than what you have, then you could become bitter, especially if you know there is or there was a chance for improvement! The way modern women live, harmonizing their families, higher education and employment is a great achievement.

Naini was once bitter about the past but not any more. After all, she says, she is not badly off compared to most of her age-mates on this planet. Some, of course, are better off than herself, but this is a reality, as we cannot all be equal and we have to accept this fact. But most of all, she is proud of her achievements. The majority of girls in her time were never allowed to enter school even to the primary level. Besides the circumstances surrounding her birth, she has done more than most could have done. Many of her friends worldwide say many young women of her age would have given up a long time ago. But she continued and is still continuing. As she says, the struggle must continue, it is not the time to give up. This expression has given her courage.

After the departure of Leshoo the previous evening, she woke up very early and went out in search of a room for herself but returned later in the evening without success. This continued for nearly two weeks, when she finally found a place. This she got through a Maasai couple, friends of hers at the Central Police Station. She had met this family through her producer during her struggle in job-seeking. They were very sympathetic to her and understood her problems.

It was during her stay at South B that Tim learnt of her new refuge and made an attempt to have her chased out of that house, but couldn't manage as the owner of the house, who was Naini's foster-father's age-mate, had protected her as his own daughter, according to Maasai tradition. And that was not all. From what Naini had explained to him of their past daily quarrels with Tim, and the scars and suffering he had caused her, he said he could not let him hurt her anymore. Being a policeman, and of a senior rank and also one who was conversant with the Maasai laws, he told Tim to go and bring Naini's parents, which was the proper procedure to conform to the Maasai customs and traditions. A girl who runs away from her husband's home because of mistreatment or misunderstandings in the family, and seeks refuge in the home of a man of the same clan or the same age-group as that of her father, is entitled to protection until the matter has been resolved by elders. Then she would go back to the husband's home. Both complainants must be given a hearing by the family and clan. On hearing this, Tim became violent and vowed that he would finish off Naini. Had it not been that the Inspector knew Tim, he could have arrested him for uttering such threatening words! But still he warned him to leave before he got angry.

'Do as I have told you before,' ordered Ole Maloi. 'Go and talk to her parents.'

Finally Tim left after the exchange with Ole Maloi. The old man later said he hoped he had put some sense into the man. He commented that the man looked more of a lunatic than a normal man. He continued to say that he knew Tim's family well and he was surprised that he was behaving like that because he came from a reputable family known for their wealth. He went on to say, 'It is a pity he misbehaved in a public place and especially in a police station.' While Tim might know his family, including himself, this did not give him the right to act like that. He assured Naini that if he did that kind of thing again, or even came to his house to try and drag Naini out, he would face the law and he would have no excuse that he hadn't been warned before.

Naini thanked Ole Maloi for his assistance and for the assurance of her protection.

That night, Naini thought of the events of that day, and promised herself that whatever happened, she would one day go and bring her children, once she had settled as she did not want them to suffer. She had no alternative at the moment but to let Tim have them for the time being, but one day, she would go and rescue her loved ones. It was hard to accept that reality of being incapable of supporting them at that time due to her financial situation and lack of permanent residence even for herself, but that's the way it was. Days became weeks, weeks turned into months! It took longer than she had anticipated. It was long but it had to be like that if she was to achieve a satisfactory and long-lasting solution. It was not easy to organize all the arrangements she had to accomplish before returning back to the countryside for the kids. One thing she had to be sure of is that she had enough money for bus fares to bring them to the city. The other thing she couldn't attempt was to bring the children while she was not in a position to support them and educate them. These criteria were vital and in this she was fully determined to attain success, for failure would mean more suffering for the children if they remained in the custody of their cruel father.

'No! no!' she said aloud. 'This won't happen.' The planning was long and difficult as she had to weigh it from all angles as overlooking any point meant complete failure and great shame. 'This must not happen,' she reinforced.

On completion of all her plans, several months after, she at last went back on her own to fetch her children. Tim did not resist; he willingly allowed her to take them as he was already fed up with them. His family hurled insults at Naini, who in turn said nothing, remembering only too well the cruelty of the mother-in-law. They provoked her, saying she had, at last come to take the children to go and sell them in Nairobi. They continued to say oh! she was going to sell her daughters one by one till all got lost in town.

One went on to ask, 'How come she has now thought of them when she had abandoned them before so as to go loitering in Nairobi, kissing men's feet instead of caring for her young ones?'

'Shame on you,' they told her.

All this she suffered painfully, thinking to herself, if they only knew how hard she had been working to arrive at this point of collecting them! But she uttered no word because she knew them well enough not to dare start any trouble. They were trying to provoke her so that Tim would have an excuse for beating her up! She thought of her index finger, which was still recovering from a previous injury inflicted by Tim and had taken several months of anguish with severe throbbing pains caused by pus. The situation was made worse by a broken bone which had not been diagnosed earlier, for which she had incurred a lot of medical expenses. Naini was bitter about this, and asked, 'How can another human being be so cruel to the extent of harming and disfiguring his wife's body until the bones rot while she is still alive?' It was unimaginable but there it was! Naini reasoned to herself that once something had happened or damage been caused, it was impossible to reverse. She never thought of any revenge.

A friend once wrote to her and told her of a proverb he learned in Madagascar: Go your way like a chameleon, one eye forward, one eye to the rear – look back to the past focusing on the happy days you have lived, and look forward with hope for a brighter future, if the present is gloomy. The proverb is very applicable to true-life situations, advising that no matter how difficult, one should never despair. Considering all the suffering of the past, Naini decided 'forward ever, backward never'. With this as her basis, her determination helped her to make a final turn which withstood all the outside influences of her relatives and friends and removed all fears.

She kept on packing the children's belongings after that. She then headed to the bus stop to take a bus to her parents' home with the children for the night, escorted by her family members. The following day she boarded a bus along with the children. They arrived in the city late that evening, tired and anxious, wondering what the future held in store for her and the children. She once again assured herself that everything would be okay. All would go according to God's plans. She finally managed to settle independently and happily thereafter on her own with her children.

Despite all her setbacks, life for Naini continued even without Tim. It was quite a big challenge for her to carry on without him. At one point, she had asked herself, was she going to be able, at her tender age, to make firm decisions on matters affecting herself and her young children? She needed courage and careful planning and to deny herself a lot of luxuries to be able to raise them and provide for their security. Naini believes it is important that one learns to manage her own problems and cope with them without involving other family members. Planning one's life can only work if one has a goal. Naini has always tried to face it on her own. During the upbringing of her children, she always tried to make them happy. Most important of all, she is sure that no one would ever mistreat them as they are capable of leading their own lives; married or unmarried. Through all her difficulties, all that she needed was determination, hope and courage. These kept Naini marching on, when most would have given up. She spent as much time as possible with her children and never neglected them. She saw them grow up to become adults now with families of their own. She is proud to see her grandchildren growing up.

Today, she can say with a lot of confidence that whatever she has achieved was through her own sweat. Naini's story is based on her own life experiences – or rather, the near truth if not absolutely accurate account of her existence. The past didn't deter her from progressing, instead, by referring to it, she got plenty of personal experiences to prove it pays to work hard. Naini has always seen herself as a person who was going to improve herself in a short period, and now she is no doubt happy of the outcome and the gains of her sweat which she has tirelessly fought for in order to achieve her ambitions.

10

WORKING FOR INDEPENDENCE

It was her two part-time jobs with the Broadcasting Corporation as an artist and radio continuity announcer that paved the way for her to start planning for her life and advancement. She admits that, had it not been for these jobs, she could have never been able to pay for her training while bringing up the children. She managed to sponsor herself for a secretarial course till she later obtained certificates. She enrolled for some English lessons and bookkeeping, though this she had done while still living at Ole Maloi's home. On completion of the courses she got a temporary job as a copy typist/receptionist in one foreign embassy and still retained her broadcasting job. It was difficult but she was determined to succeed. While still working at the foreign embassy in Nairobi, she saw an advertisement on one daily newspaper for the post of a receptionist in a large transport company, Naini put in an application and attached her photograph as was requested, and her curriculum vitae. She received a letter from the company asking her to attend an interview. The interview was so successful that after a few days she was recalled to go and start working. The job had more benefits than the two previous employments. It was also a more challenging job as it involved dealing with tourists and the public at large. She immediately wrote back confirming that she would take up the job as soon as possible.

As the years went by, her present job became more rewarding and gave her great satisfaction. At this time she was still living in the suburbs of the city. With her new job she could now afford to rent a house in a better area. She also employed a housemaid to look after the children while she was at work.

Luckily, the cost of living was not so expensive then, especially as in that area she could go to the market to buy food for about 100 shillings that would last them for nearly a month. Her children were still young then. When they started school it became more difficult, but somehow she got along with all what she had arranged. Naini never was too religious as such, but she believes in God and says God was and still is kind to her. He gave her peace of mind and most of all good health and that was more than she needed, and the strength to go through those hard times.

The following month she started her permanent job on a probation period of three months, thereafter she was confirmed. The three months passed very fast. With her permanent job there were more responsibilities, such as having to work on night shifts and leaving her young children with a mere house girl, but she had no choice.

She enjoyed working there. The other people working for the transport company were mostly mature with families, and that helped her to cope with her own situation. She realized that she was not the only one struggling; some of those people had even larger families and had to cope with situations which were even more difficult than hers. Some had children in secondary schools and in primary and they depended entirely on the little money they earned from their employment. Others earned much less than herself even though they were older than her. Naini was not the worst hit. This made her feel comfortable and a bit consoled. She now understood that she was not the only one shouldering family responsibilities.

Naini never gave up her part-time job even after getting the new job. She did, however, opt to stop the television section as she could not continue going there in the evenings. For the radio, she continued, considering that she could prepare her script at home and only go to the studio to record and leave the programme on tapes whenever she was off duty. It was taxing, but she was determined to make a living. Naini recalls that she possessed only three dresses when she got this job. And even after finding the new job, she was not able to buy others immediately. Of these three, one dress was for wearing at home and other two were for wearing when going to work, which meant washing them nearly every evening so as to have something clean to change into the following day. She had only one pair of shoes, which she had worn for so long that the sole had had to be replaced several times. This did not worry her at all; what worried her was if she was unable to buy soap to wash them. If there was one thing she disliked, it was dirt. From what she was taught by her mother and the matron at the boarding school, she knew that cleanliness is vital to stay healthy. She in fact taught on this same subject through the radio as she had to translate from the health books into the Kimaasai language. She also taught childcare after doing the translation from health books in Kimaasai. It was from these same books she herself learnt how to bring up her children as she had no guide except the books. Despite all the problems she had encountered, she reassured herself that everything will be all right.

At times Naini could not even afford to buy body cream for herself, let alone a perfume, due to her very tight budget. During those struggles, her priority was to give her children anything within her reach; they should have the best, their future must be better than her own. They should profit, unlike herself, she concluded. When she later acquired her permanent job, she asked her mother to come and help her with the children for a few days until they got used to the maid during her night shift duties. She came and she was very happy about having agreed to come.

When Tim learnt that she now has a permanent job and that the children had started going to school, he wanted to make a comeback. But she would not allow it, she simply said no. Out of that, Tim started once again creating disturbances, such as going to school during their lessons to bring the kids to her office! At one time for about three days the man wouldn't let the children study. Each morning Naini boarded the bus with the children and always dropped off to escort them to the school.

One particular time, Tim picked them up from the school at recess time without informing the headmaster of the school. Immediately after break-time, the headmaster called Naini, enquiring why she had taken the children home earlier than usual. Naini was shocked, hardly believing her ears. She had no knowledge that Tim was in town, having almost forgotten all about him as she had made a deliberate effort not to dwell on this issue. She was now very worried and had to request permission so as to go to the school to find out what had happened to them. She was in a difficult situation and didn't know where to start. For a moment she was in a state of total confusion. For once, she was trembling as her mind reflected on the past. The thought that Tim might have already driven off with the children had a big impact on her.

On arriving at the school, the other children who were interviewed said they saw a man taking them in a Land Rover. From the description, she knew straight away it was Tim. She felt stranded and became more worried, not knowing what to do next. Now the world seemed to be going upside down once again due to the appearance of Tim, whom she was certain was going to overrule her independence and destroy the peaceful atmosphere they were beginning to enjoy.

'Why can't he leave me alone in peace? Why should life be like this?' She was lost in her deep thoughts that she had said this aloud, and the headmaster was astonished to hear her talking to herself.

He interrupted her by asking, 'Like what? What is it that is worrying you?' he asked once again.

She explained to him in short about her past ordeals with Tim. He was very sympathetic and tried to comfort her. She immediately left thereafter to board a bus to her rented room at Kawangware. But that was not the end. After some days, Tim did the same thing, this time bringing all the children, including the baby, after chasing the maid.

Her employer was shocked by the sight. He gave her permission to leave and warned the man never to enter the office again. The matter was then reported to the police. Before leaving the office he cursed and insulted her, but to Naini, the insults meant nothing so long as he didn't strike her.

Another incident yet followed. Naini was going to work after her lunch when suddenly Tim appeared driving his car with intentions to crush her. On realizing this, she ran for her life. While trying to avoid the car, she fell into a gutter. She groaned in pain which was intense because she was pregnant. She started bleeding but as soon as she recovered from shock, she stood up holding *il-peres* (green grass) in both hands, which signified that she was begging for mercy. She recalls that someone motioned Tim to assist her but instead, on realizing that she was hurt, he just drove off leaving her there.

According to the Maasai tradition a handful of green grass held above the head is a sign of surrendering and seeking peace. In Maasai land, usually when two people fight and one of them plucks some green grass (*a-geru il-peres*) this will ensure that his or her opponent will desist from attacking any further as this is taken as a surrender (*a-saisho*).

Some people came rushing to her aid from the nearby bus stop and offered to take her to the hospital. She was admitted for a few days, but it did not help her as the fall had been too severe for the foetus, which was still in the early stages, so she ended up losing the child. In fact, the moment she fell, she told Tim that he had killed the child in her womb. He had not said a word, just reversed his car to avoid crushing her completely. It was not an accident; all these things he had done intentionally to hurt Naini.

Before that incident, he had told her, 'You will see what will happen to you. I notice that you are expecting a baby but I assure you that all the children you will bear are mine.' He further told her that he would come one day to take all of them, and that Naini was just like a field and it was for him to harvest everything.

There were many occasions that he had threatened to take her life until she had become accustomed to hearing it, even though, when one threatens to take your life, there is no way that your mind can stop worrying. He had tried all these things to intimidate her so that she would return to him, but had failed because Naini had made up her mind never to return to him no matter what the consequences might be. The day she went for the children, he had shown her a letter saying, 'This letter denotes I have no more powers over you, but I shall make sure that you suffer for a very long time, until you go down on your knees and apologize for your behaviour. It also indicates to me that both of us are equal and that I have no right to force you to do anything and if I disobey the orders of your lawyers they will take me to court.' He claimed that was not correct since he had paid some cows to Naini's parents so he practically owned her. Finally he had dismissed the letter, saying that her lawyer was not conversant with the Maasai traditions and customs and this was why he wrote like that. He had continued to threaten, saying unless they gave Naini a bodyguard he would not stop bothering her. Naini told herself that if she did not do what was ordered, Tim would only have another excuse to come back, and this time, he might wipe her out completely.

Another intended outcome from all these provocations was to get her fired from her job. She remembers at one time telling Tim, 'Please leave these innocent children alone because they have no knowledge of what has happened between us.' She went on to tell him that at least he had friends; what about these kids whose father was not feeding them? Should the mother also abandon them? He should be ashamed of what he was doing. He should be concerned that at least one parent saw to their well-being. After all, he himself was not abandoned by his own parents when he was young! After hearing these words, Tim just looked at her astonished and without uttering a word he walked away.

After his departure, Naini's thoughts reflected once again on the horrible past experiences of cruelty and terror. She was overcome by a feeling of insecurity as her peace and that of her children was once again being threatened by the same man as in the past. This time, she would not let him distract her from her employment.

It was during one late evening when Naini was heading to the bus stop as usual that a strange thing happened. At a corner where there were many bushes, an arm shot out, blocking her path. Two men dressed in ragged clothes appeared, and before Naini realized what was happening, the door of a car parked nearby was flung open and one stout man with a plastered hand walked towards her, leaving the others. The other two stayed by the car. One of the first two men ordered her to stop then cautioned her not to go any further. The other told her, 'You have no reason to disgrace us.'

Naini looked into the eyes of one of her former husband's henchmen, whose hand was plastered, and he grinned. Naini remembered him well because she had given him bus fare to go to hospital when he went to her office some few days before. 'I am going to work,' Naini told them, and while peering over his shoulders at the scene behind him, she noticed that Tim was sitting in the Land Rover. She immediately realized that her life was in great danger and a lot of problems awaited her.

She was then instructed to walk towards the parked vehicle, which seemed ready to take off as the engine was already running. Naini started blasting out the message in sharp fits of breath. 'You have no right to force me into that car,' she said. Naini argued that she wanted to go to her place of work as she was on night shift, and that she didn't need a lift. One of the men just laughed at her. The man laughed again, showing an abundance of white teeth in a broad grin that stretched the skin on his face and exposing his black gum, revealed two missing teeth in the centre of his lower jaw. The young man was in no hurry to act. Then the other ordered Naini to get into the Land Rover. 'You will not get away with this,' she warned them once again.

In the car, her hands were tied and she was made to sit between two men in front of the car. The man who had earlier ordered Naini to go into the car sat in the back seat. It was only then that Naini learnt that Tim was the ringleader as

143

the others referred to him as 'chief'. Naini could not imagine that Tim, who was the father of her children, could truly arrange for her killing! At this point, she nearly fainted. Instead of heading towards Nairobi, the car was driven towards Kabete. For a while Naini was lost in her thoughts; this was like a dream. She could not believe that this was actually happening to her. She realized it was not a dream and it was actually true she was being kidnapped!

'I am going to throw you into the escarpment, which will crush your bones into pieces,' Tim said to her. As if that was not enough he went on to tell her, 'It could be days before they find your remains, and no one would ever know what had actually happened to you. After all, no one saw us when we picked you up.'

All this time Naini was trying to stay calm even though her heart was beating very fast due to fear. Inside her mind she was trying to find a way to escape but found none as she was sitting trapped in the middle of the gang. As soon as the car started increasing speed, she realized that the man meant what he had said. She started screaming at the top of her voice to attract attention from passers-by, but the car was speeding so fast that no one paid any attention!

For Naini, this was going to be the end of her life as the man had already threatened before that he would take her life. For once, Naini was in a desperate situation and in a state of shock. Although she tried to overcome her fears by assuring herself that she would still escape, this was beyond her capability. She prayed for some miracle to happen. She even imagined some police coming to her rescue and arresting the man and his gang and releasing her to freedom and safety – but to her disappointment, none of this was forthcoming. She continued screaming at the top of her voice as the car sped away. For many miles there was no sign of any policemen and none of the passers-by dared to stop the speeding vehicle in case the occupants had guns. To many, she imagined, it looked like a getaway car after a hold-up in some kind of robbery. She continued screaming until she lost her voice.

144

It was just by sheer luck, as they reached somewhere on the outskirts of town, that she saw from a distance that there were some traffic police by the road blocks, and on realizing this, she got set to jump out of the car and run for dear life if the opportunity arose. On noticing the presence of the police, the group took swift action by loosening the rope with which they had tied her hands.

Naini then realized that this was her only chance for survival and took the opportunity to scream even louder in order to attract the attention of the policemen. She managed to get hold of the steering wheel of the car. During the struggle, the car zigzagged from one side of the road to the other, prompting the police to notice that there was a problem. They then signalled the car to stop, but Tim refused. In another desperate attempt, Naini smashed the windscreen of the car with a pair of pliers which was lying in the glove compartment the very minute her hands were free!

By this time, the man and his group were nervous and furious as they watched their kidnapping plan fail. In annoyance one man hit Naini across the face, saying she was too loud-mouthed, and ordered her to stop screaming otherwise he was going to slap her once again. This did not stop her screaming as she knew that, either way, they would continue with their intention and, in any case, she had nothing to lose.

As the car went on swaying from one side of the road to the other, they continued to struggle for control of the car. But they realized that they were not going to get anywhere, first, because of the broken windscreen and second, because the police might have noted down the car's registration number due to the fact that they were driving fast and for failing to stop when signalled by the traffic police. The broken windscreen also caused the car to slow down because there was a strong wind. Despite all the efforts that Tim put in that instant to correct the situation, the police realized that there was something amiss and they decided to follow the car. Since they were on foot, they chose to ask for a lift from a passing car.

They chased the car until they caught up with them,

145

passed them and then they abruptly parked just in front of them. This time, Tim had no choice but to stop the car. The two policemen jumped out of the car with their pistols drawn! Tim and his gang stayed inside the Land Rover waiting for them. The policemen headed immediately towards the parked vehicle, and asked Tim 'Why did you refuse to stop at the road block?' To which Tim answered, 'I am sorry I did not notice that you were asking me to stop.'

'Why is this woman screaming?' demanded the second policeman.

Tim then started to explain that Naini was his wife who was unwell and that he was taking her to her parents in the Rift Valley. He was lying, of course.

In turn, Naini, who had jumped out of the car the moment it had stopped, could hardly wait without interrupting to narrate all that had taken place, step by step. She told the policemen, 'This man [Tim] is lying that I am sick, I am crying because this man and his group intend to kill me, and so I was screaming to attract attention for help because they kidnapped me by forcing me into the car and tied my hands.' By then Naini's eyes were swollen with tears. Naini further revealed she was on her way to work when this happened. The three of them were going to kill her at the escarpment and then throw her at the *maboromoko* cliff, where her body was going to rot without anyone ever finding out the truth or even knowing how it happened. She went on to tell them that if they wanted to know more, they should just contact Ngong Police Station, where she had made several statements before this incident of his intended fatal action.

On hearing this, Tim lost his temper and said, yes it was true but he meant her no harm. 'I just wanted to return her to her parents because we had disagreed and I couldn't leave her in Nairobi'. He went on to say. 'According to our Maasai traditions we have to go to the elders and have this issue discussed to determine who is at fault.'

The police asked Tim, 'Mr Tim, do you know that according to the law you have no right to take her against her will? We must go to the station.'

146

At the station, Tim was told to leave Naini alone and instead go and bring the parents so that the matter could be discussed by the elders from both families. He was then warned not to interfere with Naini otherwise he would be charged.

As for Naini, she was escorted to her place of work in the town and advised to report any further harassment or interference from Tim.

Naini was very grateful for what the policemen did for her, especially the trouble they took in driving her all the long way to drop her just in front of her place of work, ensuring her safety. It was not until after 7.00 p.m. that she came to the end of the traumatic ordeal. While they were driving towards the town, Naini had explained to them that she was supposed to report on duty at 4.00 p.m. and her worry was what her employer would tell her the following day! On arrival, one of the policemen walked with her to the office to explain in brief of what had happened, after which they left. Naini was still in too much of a state of shock to explain.

After their departure, Naini settled down a bit then resumed duties. Her colleagues told her that they knew that she must have been in some kind of trouble. Knowing her as a punctual person they had wondered why she hadn't phoned to tell him that she would be arriving late. Surely she couldn't fail to come or telephone, or if she was ill, she could ask somebody to call on her behalf.

That same night while on duty, Naini tried to forget the events of the day, but to no avail, even after assuring herself of the laws of the land. She contemplated a great deal about her life, her family and clan and said to herself, 'After all why should I worry, I cannot lie, therefore I must only tell them the truth, and my final decision.' It was her life and not theirs which was affected and she was the one bearing that burden and facing all the hardships. Why was she born, when she could not even enjoy the life she was born to enjoy because someone is going to shorten her life, just because he thought he had bought her like an object?

These were the thoughts that flashed through Naini's

mind, and when she came to the end of her contemplation, she still wept bitterly. She was so overwhelmed by grief that she could hardly even carry on her office work. Her colleagues were understanding and helpful as most of them were older men and women who had passed through a lot of hardships of one kind or another. This was one of the thoughts that consoled Naini and also knowing that she was not alone in having been forced to marry someone she didn't love at a tender age, before she could really understand the realities of life. They comforted her, advising her to take it easy and to remain self-confident.

She then resolved to keep strong so as to have a strong weapon to confront her enemies. The greatest defence was to keep her mind intact, not to cloud it with too many worries. The brain, she believed, was the engine of the whole body and once it was overworked, it would cease to function. So one must help it run and keep running at a moderate speed.

'I must stay strong whatever happens,' she said to herself, even though deep down, Naini feared a curse from the family. But she had to choose either to love herself and to consider herself first before her foster-father and mother, or live with the man and let herself be destroyed. She decided to consider herself before the rest, and that she would never return to the man. This was her final decision. She could not continue living in fear and depression, because the consequence of such a life was detrimental to her mind. If she went crazy, neither the man nor her family would maintain her for long as she would become a public liability and a public nuisance. No one would love her any more. This was why she had to stand on her own feet, as she loved herself and she would work harder to better the lives of her young ones so that they do not encounter the same situation later.

Naini sat down and once again wrote a long letter to her family explaining from the very beginning all that she had been through until this particular moment, and also informing them of her decision never to return to the man. She thought of a Kiswahili proverb once told by a friend which states '*kurudi kinyume ina majuto mabaya sana*' (the consequence of revoking one's decision can be great). In the meantime, she had to find a permanent solution to her endless disturbances.

Her family, on hearing the sad news, informed the clan, and after a meeting they declared to support her fully by all means possible. At the same time her foster-father wrote a letter to Naini's lawyer explaining to him that in fact he was in the midst of taking Naini away because the man had never completed payment of the dowry as he had promised and never performed all the ceremonies as requested by the clan.

Nick was Naini's esteemed friend with whom she confided her family's problems. Many a time she wrote to him to seek advice on how to resolve many of her endless problems, and luckily enough, he was always there. Every one needs a friend, not only during happy moments, but also in times of crises and crucial times of ones life.

When the world around you seems to be boiling like a volcano discharging ashes and smoke from high and spreading lava over the lowland, burning everything in its path, when one is hurt due to mistreatment when one's surroundings became unstable one is bound to feel insecure. But there is a way. Nick was always a good listener and wrote to her regularly to acknowledge her sad letters. His counselling gave her hope to continue her struggle and she gained the self-confidence to learn and live with the reality of her ruined childhood. His soothing, encouraging brotherly words made an impact on her and she gained the ability to resist changes of any kind.

Nick was by then working at the United Nations Headquarters, he now lives and works in Kenya; they have both maintained a high respect for one another.

Dear Nick [Naini later wrote to her friend]
I want to relate to you about the correspondence which took place way back before my final decision to leave Tim, those

149

written to my family as well as those written to my lawyer and their replies, and those written to my former employer.

Dear Sir,
Pending the divorce case in court, I wish to seek protection during office hours as I feel that my job is at stake due to the recent disturbances caused by Tim. My lawyers have already written to him (Tim) to refrain him from interfering with me pending the decision.
Thanking you for your understanding in this disturbing matter.
Yours faithfully,
Naini
(copy of the letter given to her stepfather for information and action)

The following is a letter from her stepfather to her employer in support:

Dear Sir,
Re: *Naini*
The above named lady is my daughter. She is undergoing a course in Nairobi and she had been working in your establishment, but lately I came to understand that her husband had written to you asking you to get her sacked from work.
I have to assure you that my daughter does not receive any support from her husband at all. She is paying the course fees alone through what she gets from her employment.
I have spoken to her husband but he seems to be not willing his wife to continue her course but I rejected his objection. It would be very much appreciated if you could let her continue working in your firm.
Thanks
Yours faithfully,
Olomunyak

Naini wrote as follows to the lawyer:

1) Married for about six years. The marriage was an arranged one with pressure from parents, I was forced to marry him. However I was prepared to show loyalty and faithfulness under all circumstances, if it was not due to his unfaithfulness to me and mistreatment.

2) The unfaithfulness took the nature of public scandal because he was involved in a case which appeared in the papers and which completely left me with insurmountable shock. If he was a faithful husband how could he leave me and the children and go and have a good time in town.

3) Never for once has he cared about our children. Whatever money he has got, he squandered it all alone in town and comes home drunken. We have four children, how can one expect me to educate and feed four children out of a meagre pocket of a wife? And yet this is what I have been doing all the years (about four years) with utmost patience. I have to earn the money, come and pay rent, feed the children, clothe the children, pay the maid and pay their school fees. The husband sits at home when he can work but out of pride, he is unwilling to work for little pay. How long can one go on showing patience?

4) And yet that is no sign of goodwill from my side. Instead of some kind of appreciation, I have constantly been the object of placating his anger. There is hardly a day when he refrains from throwing bitter and angry words at me. He has beaten me so often and even marred my body. I have had to go to hospital for long treatment and all at my own cost.

5) Instead of respecting the work I am doing, he doesn't hesitate to go to the office where I work and create rowdy scenes there. He has gone so far as to beat me at the very office where I earned the

money to feed him and our children. We have had to go lately to a police station because of such a public brawl in the office.

6) I am constantly living in a state of fear and I have no concentration in my work. Neither have I got the peace to sit down and be happy with my children. More than twice he has been intimidating me that he will take my life and go and throw me where my body cannot be found. This intimidation more than anything else has forced me to seek your assistance right away.

This is Naini's letter to her stepfather, forwarding a copy of the above letter and original letter (below) from her lawyer.

My dear father,
I am writing to inform you that I have now made up my decision to engage a lawyer to take up my case because life with Tim has completely become unbearable that I cannot withstand it any longer. Enclosed with the above is the list of what is required by the lawyer to enable him to take action.

What we require

1) Is there a marriage between Naini and Tim celebrated under the Maasai customary Law:

    (i) If the dowry is a prerequisite under the Maasai custom; has it been paid,
    (ii) Have the other customary formalities necessary for a valid marriage been performed?
    (iii) What are the formalities necessary under Maasai custom to constitute a valid marriage.

2) Assuming there is a valid marriage under Maasai customary Law, what are the grounds for dissolution of such marriage and what are the necessary formalities.

The reply to the lawyer's note from Naini's stepfather Olomunyak read:

Dear Sirs,

I am aware that my daughter Naini has employed you to defend her.

I am also aware that she filed a case of divorce against Mr Tim.

My opinion to this is that, I have allowed Naini to divorce her husband with effect from the date of this letter, for the following reasons:

(a) Naini for several occasions has been beaten and hurt.

(b) She has been kept as a slave but NOT a happy house-wife.

(c) She married Tim early sixties; and after some years the dowry was paid immediately after their quarrel had ensued. By this time Naini had already made up her decision to leave Tim.

(d) She has for the last 4 years and over been and still is supporting her own children in everything including their education as well as Tim. Tim was bankrupt and jobless for the whole of that period.

(e) The dowry is not complete yet. Still one more heifer and a sheep unpaid.

(f) At their marriage in the early sixties, I asked Tim to wed in a church but he refused.

(g) I am always being abused by Tim and cannot tolerate his abuse any longer.

(h) I had warned Tim on several occasion to live a good life with Naini but all were in vain.

(i) The last ceremony known as "ENTUNORE" which marks as a wedding ring had *never* been performed which of course indicates that Tim and Naini are JUST living as a boy friend and girl friend BUT NOT as a husband and a wife.

With all these reasons Naini must be freed from slavery so as to live a happy life like any other human being.

If anything else is needed or required by you please contact me direct or through Naini.

For your information, I am forwarding to Tim a copy of this letter.

Now before the hearing of this case merely because it is me who let them marry but NOT the court or any body else. Still it is me to make them divorce one another. So I declare that my daughter is NO LONGER Tim's wife.

Yours faithfully,
Olomunyak

The above letters are all dated over 20 years ago, and were preserved by Naini.

The letter below is addressed to Naini by her father and dated 12/8/70

Dearest Daughter,

I am in receipt of your letters and all are fully understood. Secondly, I am sorry to have heard the dangers you faced in a motor accident. God be with you.

Now, you better concentrate for while, I will try my means and ways I could to see that you lead a good life. In the meantime, you have my blessings to go ahead without further hesitation.

I couldn't be able to come because of much work that I have at home. Please give the attached letter to your lawyer.

With love,
Olomunyak

And that was how Naini at last won the battle. Naini wanted to celebrate her accomplishment, but before doing so, she first of all had to make peace and get her family's blessings. She at last made peace with her family after all that suffering, as they also realized that she was not just letting herself go and appreciated her determination to better her life. Her deeds made them confide in her. When Tim next arrived in the countryside from Nairobi, none of her family members had time for him and they no longer wanted to listen to his endless stories. Tim was a good talker, he could plan things, but none ever took off. He was not a man of action, but a talker. He tried to campaign to win support from the elders of the village, but since they had learnt of what had taken place, no one favoured him any more. The fact that he had the evil intention to kill Naini was enough. A man wanting to kill his wife, the mother of his children! This was shocking to everybody. Thereafter, he never went back to discuss what had taken place.

The community knew that he was jealous that Naini could make it without him to support the children and to care for herself. It seems that it hurts men to see a woman making more progress on her own. A man, in a way, will feel happier when a woman cannot make it on her own. Then he will proudly say, 'Look at her now, she was living well because of me and now she cannot even get food to eat and cannot afford to dress herself.'

On the other hand, if a woman succeeds, the man feels disgraced.

Naini's children were deeply affected by the violence and daily family clashes between the parents especially one day when he hit her on the head with a high-heeled shoe and also the incident when he threw the bottle at her face and she injured her palm very seriously. He had sworn to destroy her beauty. In one of the many fights, one of the children had been hit at a tender age when trying to come to her aid! This left the child with a lot of fear for a very long time. They were undeterred by the bleak conditions around them following these clashes that even at one time rendered them homeless. On two occasions, Naini ended up in hospital, returning each time to the house with stitches. This was unforgettable.

Today Naini wants the world to know that many young girls of tender age are mistreated, denied their human rights and no one lifts a finger to their defence in many developing countries. The United Nations should impose a law on all member states, she thinks, to restrain parents all over the world from selling their girl children – either by introducing them into prostitution or by forced marriages – and enlighten them on the consequences of such marriages. The children should be left alone to choose their future partners and to have their own liberty to make decisions, she says. Parents must know that it is the girl's or boy's future which is at stake and not theirs. Children are not disposable objects. A parent may comment but cannot force a child to have the same kind of friends.

Her word to the less unfortunate ones is, and this is especially directed to the single young mothers, 'the struggle must continue. If you have children, don't abandon them, don't panic if ever something like this happens to you, or if you are forced by circumstances to divorce. Ask yourself this question: 'Supposing he had died of an accident or sickness, what would I do?' Don't panic, stand firm and tell yourself you are here to remain with your loved ones. You must work hard to establish your existence by all means. Never give up in life, the struggle must continue until you achieve the goal and harvest the fruits of your sweat. Rest assured that no one else can better your condition of living except your own self. One should never despair because there is always a way of solving the problems and this can only come about if you keep your mind intact. Whatever is worrying you, always assure yourself that you can find a solution to it. Most important of all is if you have good health, count yourself luckier than a millionaire with all the money in the world.

Don't harm yourself by creating more reasons for worries or trying to take your life just because someone forced you into marriage or because a loved one has left you. This is a cowardly way of solving the problem. Face it, no matter how difficult it is. If he can find someone, you too can find someone. It is not easy but you can get over it. This calls for a lot of determination and courage and you soon get over it. It is only you, and you alone, who can ruin yourself or improve your conditions and work your way up the ladder to your success. Always try to keep your head above the waters then you cannot sink. Pray, hope, and most of all have a goal to aim at. Then you can steer your boat to a safe landing. One's future should not be contaminated by a monstrous present or past. The size of your thinking, your goals, your attitudes, your very personality is formed by your environment. There is nothing as bad as wondering aimlessly, hoping opportunity will somehow, someday, hit you in the face.

Naini didn't let pessimism dictate, and didn't surrender to suppressive forces, but instead she believed in working hard and tirelessly to make ends meet because success is achieved through hard work.

There are many young women who are victims of circumstances and who might not have the courage and resistance to face the hard situation in life the way Naini herself resisted, without at any one time giving up despite a lot of suffering, beatings, hard conditions of living and the struggle of bringing up her young children single-handedly at her tender age. When Naini got her first child at the age of 14, she was a child bringing up another child! At times she would cry because of depression as she had no knowledge of a child's upbringing. Each morning, she prayed and thanked the Lord for yet another day and hoped that that day was going to be brighter than the one before. Day after day she yearned for the best while knowing that the struggle must continue if she had to succeed in this cruel world.

Naini eventually opted to send her children to boarding schools as a result of the many disturbances caused by Tim. They went through their primary education and later proceeded to different secondary schools in Kenya. Throughout their education, Tim never contributed a cent. He never looked back to assist in the children's upbringing. All in all, she brought them up without any financial assistance even from her own family. She was proud to have managed to bring them up on her own. This made her feel relieved she had gone through the most delicate part and that the children would now be independent to choose for themselves what to do and without anyone ever forcing them into marriage.

All her children are more or less self-sufficient now. After their high school, they chose not to continue and instead took various courses and are now working, are independent and contributing to society. Naini feels happy as this has relieved her of some responsibilities of having to cater for them and hopes this will continue. It is now up to them to seize this opportunity and make the best out of their education by putting their talents to use so as to improve their abilities and to seek a prosperous future for themselves and their families.

Although there are also women who are negligent and who do not take their family responsibilities seriously, Naini has no objection if the male partner requests the wife to undertake certain responsibilities towards the family's wellbeing if she is working.

The majority of women suffer through no fault of their own due to mistreatment from men. This is worse for housewives who depend entirely on a working husband who may decide not to show up at home after pay day or after squandering all his earnings. This brings a lot of sorrows, especially if the couple have children to maintain and worst still the woman could end up in hospital with high blood pressure from depression and frustration.

In times of hardships, we need all our health and our strength to adequately respond to the challenges of life that come our way.

Naini quotes a saying once told by a friend: 'It is better to teach a child a trade than to give him/her charity.' Her recommendation is, no matter how comfortable you can be, if you have a chance you should learn a skill because you can never know when you will need it. It is wiser to equip yourself to be ready to work at any time. Assist someone else too to learn a trade. Rarely do women abandon their children, only in extreme cases whereby they are completely without means and ways of supporting them. Most women work hard to see that their children don't go without food and if possible put them through education. She does not mean to say that men do not care about their children but the point she is trying to put across is they look at things in a different angle. This is why it is crucial for young ladies to acquire skills if possible for future use. This also applies to young men who will one day take up the responsibilities of running their own homes and bringing up families.

Nobody knows about tomorrow, so it is wise for us to prepare ourselves for whatever may come our way. Her word to the housewives is this: Don't neglect yourselves. There are many refreshing activities which will keep boredom at bay. Please don't overwork your brains, instead, you should nourish it by giving it time to rest in order to work for you tomorrow. Everyone needs his/her own existence, so save yourselves by reducing excessive worrying which will not serve any useful purpose. When the brain is overworked, the body mechanism is impaired, resulting in bad job performance. It will continue to deteriorate until it is completely incapable of making decisions, and that is bad. Save it so that it will work for you till the end of your life in perfect condition.

11

NAINI'S HOUSE

Naini's job with the transport company progressed well after working with them for one year. She was transferred to another department, where she proceeded to work for several years. It was while working with that company that she conceived the idea of trying to save some money to buy a small place of her own where she would live in her old age. It took her a very long time to implement this and she was afraid of being unable to meet her mortgage repayments, considering that she was still trying to cater for her children's education and their maintenance. Due to all these factors, it took her a long time to accumulate enough funds for a deposit. The other setback for advancement was the lack of security to enable her to borrow money from banks.

Naini's best memories are focused on the time she was allocated a house in Nairobi by an estate agent, Mr Kamau, whose manager she was introduced to by a friend called David who was from a foreign country and was himself in the housing industry.

It was on a Monday morning while she was reading a Kenyan daily journal that an advertisement on houses for sale struck her. For many years, she had always wanted to have a place of her own, but due to the many commitments of bringing up the kids it had not been possible. She had not been able to fulfil her lifetime dream until this particular day. She showed the article to her friend, who in turn told her to go and see Mr Kamau so as to fill in an application form.

She told David that she might not qualify as she might not

even be able to raise the ten per cent deposit required as down payment. She had no security to guarantee a loan from a bank and moreover there would be stamp duty and legal fees on top of the price to be paid before she could be considered.

To her surprise David came up immediately with a bright idea: he assured her that it was not impossible (a thing she had never thought of herself) since the house itself would have a title deed and the bank could hold it as a security. If she failed to meet the repayments, they would then sell the house to recover their money. He further suggested to her that she should also request her employer to issue her with an attestation indicating that she was actually working and specifying her monthly income. And if possible, she should also borrow part of the money from the employer and the rest from her own little savings, and then David would assist her to raise the balance.

There it was, the plan was concluded. Had it not been for his bright idea she thinks she could never have succeeded. This project coincided with the completion of her children's secondary school education. She was so happy about this development and prayed that all would go as planned.

After going through all the administrative process of the documents from both the bank and the estate agent and registration through a lawyer, she celebrated her achievement. This was a memorable moment in her life, as she turned to another chapter, a brighter one.

Nowadays, Naini is even more touched when she reflects on those wonderful moments and those true friends who wanted to see her rise and whose wise advice inspired her to work tirelessly through and towards her long-overdue project and whose support created a strong influence on its accomplishment.

For further encouragement, a friend once told her, 'Life is not the days passed but the days we remember. Sweet memories make it easier to look forward to the inevitable how far or near it may be.' In another letter he went further to encourage her by saying, 'Naini you are a brave young woman and you will beat it all and with your determination, strong will, you will succeed. Don't forget that everyday we are growing older and we shall be approaching the critical age some day and many small and big problems are coming. Please hold your head and follow your way, stick to your target. Naini, remember this, one's future should not be contaminated by a monstrous past or present.'

Through her own experience of acquiring her little house despite the many restrictions here and there, Naini wishes to request the banks and employers to assist the workers and especially the lower-class salary earners to enable them to acquire property. When the workers feel secure, their job performance improves. The banks should not make it impossible for them. After all, the majority of upper-class workers and rich people don't always have money to buy property in cash. Most of all, most people rent their houses to be able to meet the monthly repayments for a certain period until the interest rate is no longer too high. The bank in the meantime can retain the title deed until such time as agreed in the sale contract and the purchaser redeems the said title.

On the other hand, if the purchaser doesn't abide by the conditions, e.g. due to unemployment, then the bank concerned can re-rent the house on behalf of the purchaser until such time as the title is redeemed or the purchaser is once again capable of making the repayments himself/herself. Re-allocation of such houses to new buyers should not arise. It should be avoided as this will deprive that buyer the right of ever owning a house having put all his/her savings as a deposit.

Shelter is a necessity for every individual as it guarantees security. Naini says she would appreciate it very much more if the bank advanced her money to buy or build a home for her family than lend her money to buy a car which, in times of unemployment, would need more money to run it. The family could not sleep inside it when it was raining and keep their few belongings locked up in security. Unlike the house: one could live in it, and at the same time re-rent one part to generate some little income which could be paid towards the outstanding loan or for the maintenance of the family.

It was again Naini's own determination which at last helped her to fulfil her long overdue dream of years ago when finally she acquired a loan for a house. The other odd jobs, such as modelling, which she enjoyed so much, and the advertisements shown in the magazines and cinemas, also contributed to her development. Even though most of these jobs were voluntary they did at least raise her morale and helped shape her to what she is today. She also took part in a film to assist a friend in the film business, free of charge. Most of all, she felt useful to the society.

When she reflects on the past Naini smiles even though she knows that she never actually lived for herself, but she felt happier whenever she was able to help someone else, which is not always the case! She says it is better sharing with others, though some people would rather throw away food than give it to someone dying of hunger!

In Africa, we always have extended families and the Maasai community is no exception. This is still true, because despite the passage of time, the Maasai still maintain a spiritual link with their roots. The history of our community is passed on from one generation to another. The responsibilities of the community especially include taking care of aged people. Naini is proud that her community has managed to retain most of the cultural heritage. She herself has never abandoned her responsibilities. Besides bringing up her own children in those difficult conditions, she used to assist some of her relatives who were in a worse situation than she was. She had determination, which some didn't have, or rather she felt she had had a better chance in her later years to improve herself, through her own initiative. At times, she was amazed at how she managed, but she knows the answer – because she denied herself many things for the sake of others, the less fortunate and the more needy than herself. Her foster-father married a second wife, who also bore many children besides her mother's own children. She even went to the extent of paying school fees for some of her brothers. Whenever she had a little money to spare, she helped them. She wished she could do more, so as to see all her relatives happy and settled in better conditions of living, but unfortunately it was not possible. But so far she knows, they remember and appreciate the little things she has done for them.

At times Naini has been harsh to them, especially to those relatives who just decide to board a bus to come to Nairobi without any warning, to come and demand financial assistance. Instead of writing a letter to explain the problem, and the amount involved, they decide to come even in the middle of the month when the pocket has a hole! Now Naini will be faced by more expenses, not only the expense of school fees that her aunt has come for but also the bus fares and feeding an extended family. One Monday morning, her aunty arrived with her little son who has been chased away from school because of non-payment of school books and school fees.

While having tea, and exchanging news as customary, she then broke the news, which was what Naini wanted to hear so that she could start working on it. She reasoned it out with her like this: How much money did you pay for your transport? She said 'One hundred and twenty for me and sixty for the boy.' And where did you get this money? She replied that she had borrowed it. And how much is the school fees and the money to buy books? She replied, 'Three hundred and fifty shillings.'

"Now my dear aunty, do you know how much it is going to cost me now to clear all your debts?' Naini asked. She said, 'Three hundred and fifty.' Naini nearly screamed at her but she held her tongue, and asked the little boy to note it down: Transport coming and back, 360 plus 180 to be refunded to *Parsaloi* family plus 350 for school fees and the books! The whole thing was going to cost 860 shillings.

'Oh my God!' the aunty exclaimed.

Then Naini told her that had she just phoned or written a letter, she could have saved some of the money for herself and done something else with it! They both agreed with Naini and promised never to do that again.

164

Although Tim's relatives sometimes called her *paashe*, Naini never actually identified any of the cows given to her that evening after the marriage. This was just a name. Oh! come to think of it, she knows she should have demanded to see the cows and driven them to her home for her son's sake. After all, he is named after Tim and the clan approve of this. Her sons are entitled to land as well as cattle. The cattle will be used some day to pay dowry when they decide to marry. Perhaps it is too late now because Tim has long since remarried and has several other children with his new wife. Oh yes! but as the Maasai say in a proverb *imeimulaa esile olkujita* – meaning a debt will always be a debt, literal translation: it will not be covered by grass. It is not really a debt but a right for the children to inherit. But she will go and ask for them, one day.

For many years Naini lived a different life on her own in the company of her children. After getting free from Tim, she did not commit herself to any man due to the love for her children, who were still too young. She met many nice people, but due to the past experience, she avoided having a close relationship with any man. She had social contacts, but that was all.

The reason were these: if she ever got seriously involved with somebody, to the extent of marrying him, then she would be bound to give him children. And how sure was she that he was going to take care of them all? At the same time, she kept in mind that he might not treat them equally, and especially the children she was going to bring along. These thoughts made her retreat and hold back her emotions. At the beginning, it might work, but once she had a child with him, all might change, his love may become focused on his own children and not the others! She was afraid as she would be the sufferer because her love was for all of them and not for one or two!

It was on one Tuesday evening after nearly ten years that Naini reunited with an old school friend Neliyio. After school, they had lost contact when Naini was given away. Neliyio had learnt from another former schoolmate that Naini was now living at Ngong and had been given her address and her office telephone number. That very day, she had called the office but was informed that Naini was at home.

Neliyio arrived at Naini's house late that evening and found her lying in bed unable to move due to aches from beatings by Tim. This incident was the last of such beatings during which Naini's child had also suffered, as mentioned before. She sympathized with her and was very disappointed that someone could do such a thing to another just because of marriage! She swore never to get married if those were the consequences. Neliyio was let free by her parents to continue with her education. Unlike Naini, Neliyio was not forced into marriage. Her parents couldn't possibly force her to do what she didn't want. They wanted her to continue with her teaching job and if possible get married one day to someone she loved. They told her if she did not want to get married, she could just have children after her training because she would be able to bring them up on her own from her income.

She stayed with them for several days to try to comfort her best friend Naini. Neliyio was sad to have met her friend in such a condition after so many years of separation since the days in secondary school. Naini remembered her girlfriend as a kind-hearted person. During their schooling, she had helped her many times and was always very understanding. Besides their separation, their relationship had remained unchanged although now they were trying to renew contact this time as grown-ups in their twenties.

That night, they had talked about many things, including life experiences, families and last but not least their former friends during their youth. With honesty and warmth, Neliyio shared her own tale with her dear friend Naini about the good and the bad times, the late nights of dancing into dawn, the cinemas, all the great people she had met, whom she loved and cherished and most of all about the interesting places she visited in Nairobi whenever she had time to spare

166

in order to forget some of her troubles and to kill boredom.
After standard eight (KAPE), she had got a chance to work as an untrained teacher this meant she was already ahead of Naini, who had just started working. She told her of her experience in the teaching profession.

Naini, for her part, also narrated to Neliyio all that which had transpired between her and Tim since she arrived in the big city, and her perseverance during her so-called traditional marriage which had left her at the mercy of traditional beliefs and omens, and the consequences which led her to at last run away to the city to try to better her life on her own, her struggle to study and the bringing up of her kids as a single parent and about her complaints to her family. She specifically told her nearly in sequence as much as she could remember ... How the member of Tim's family mistreated her and how she was separating from Tim for good.

Naini was very happy to have met Neliyio as she had wanted to tell someone who would understand her and she was the only one she could confide in. Her friend was patient and let her continue her tale without interruption. At the end of her story, she excused herself as she felt that she was beginning to bore her with her sad stories, and changed the subject. She went on to discuss their good old days in school.

Then Neliyio asked, 'Do you still remember what we used to eat? And how we served it?'

'Oh yes! How could I possibly forget that!' replied Naini.

'Do you still remember our school menu?' demanded Neliyio.

'Oh yes!' Naini said.

Neliyio said she had nearly forgotten about that part of their life after all those years.

Then they talked about a girl who got pregnant at school Nashipai, who was much older than them, gave birth in their dormitory to a baby girl. Naini asked 'You mean the tall, dark-skinned girl?'

'Oh yes!' replied Neliyio. The way she said it was so funny that they both started laughing despite all the pains Naini had.

Nashipai had tried to hide her pregnancy all that period and even the matron never knew about it until that very last minute when the baby was actually being born! The matron was very sad because she had trusted that girl so much that, at one time she had even been given as an example of a perfect girl.

Neliyio then took over the conversation, adding that Nashipai had difficulties eating the school meals. 'You remember our meals consisted of *ugali* with one potato, a piece of meat and some soup or stew? These were served by older girls in turns as there was a duty roster to be followed each week. For us younger ones, we had no access to serving the meals, leave alone going near the food when it was being served! We practically never ate any meat! Most of the time only soup and bones! For those who had the chance to serve, they ate the cream of everything. Enough *ugali*, several pieces of meat and above all they put enough sauce for themselves. For the rest of the older girls, they could not complain because they also did the same when it was their turn. But their lot was not as bad as the one of younger girls.

'When I started to serve the food, I too did exactly the same thing as the others used to do. As a cover-up to make everyone happy, my partner and I dug a hole inside the *ugali*, making it like a bowl and then filled it with meat. We then turned it upside down to hide the meat then added a little soup and a piece of meat on the plate! As usual, we also did the same thing for our friends. For the newcomers, they were happy as they did not know this trick. One could only learn these tricks the day when you were promoted by the big girls to serve food.

'Beside eating *ugali*, there were days when we ate maize and beans full of black tiny weevils, which were nearly part of the ingredients remember?'

Naini once again went on to tell her best friend Neliyio that she was giving her her confidence as she has always wanted to tell somebody. 'Please don't misunderstand me, Neliyio, having told you about the circumstances that which surrounded my own arranged marriage, this does not mean that young girls are only exploited through marriage, but this is the principal point in most African countries and other Third World countries. 'There are other families who practically sell their children, perhaps due to poverty, by introducing them into prostitution in order to earn money to feed on. This happens in countries such as India and many other underdeveloped countries.

'Some women too, can be cruel to their children, but such circumstances are very rare. Most mothers can make sacrifices even to the extent of staying hungry so that their children can eat. We should always take part to protect our young ones at all cost.'

Naini remembered watching a bird building a nest, working very hard. The more she watched it, the more she admired it for its efforts to build a home for her young ones. It was admirable to see that they think of the protection of their young ones long before the eggs are laid. Birds are intelligent too. The bird had worked tirelessly to gather the materials necessary to build! Each time she flew away, she returned bringing green grass, using her bill. This went on for several days till she at last completed it. She laid the eggs and when they hatched, she started once again making the same long trips, this time in search of food to make sure they had enough to eat until they were able to take care of themselves. The animals too do the same thing for their young ones, so why should the human race become cruel to their young?

Naini continued to tell Neliyio how after she had secured a permanent job, she had to contribute to the economy for the well-being of her entire family. For her children she tried to set a good example to them by giving them education and she had alerted them of the many obstacles which they would encounter in a later stage when they were not under her care. She had told them of the consequences if one is lazy and doesn't take school seriously. She went on to say, 'I know I was a little hard on them at times but to be both mother and father at that tender age was quite a difficult task for me and also taking into consideration the inadequate finances to support myself and the children whilst facing the many changes on my own'

All in all she looked to a brighter future. Having come that long way she felt it was not now that she was going to give up hope. 'It pays to work hard in all that you do because you will at last get self-satisfaction and you can rest assured that one day you will harvest the fruits of your sweat, because success is earned through hard work,' she said to Neliyio.

Although most of her marriage life was spent in tears, bitterness and a lot of suffering, Naini still worked hard to establish her own existence and that of her young ones as she couldn't back away from the responsibilities of a mother. She admitted to Neliyio that she was not a perfect mother, but she felt she had set a fine example to her children, unlike some ladies she had met in her life, some who had more problems than herself and who could not face the reality of life and live to their expectations.

12

THE STORY OF NAREYRO

Like Naini, Nareyro too was born at Oloropil four years later. Since their biological father was not permitted to marry their mother due to clanism, they were then left to live with their grandmother. Despite this setback of not succeeding in marrying her, their biological father continued secretly meeting their mother until the birth of Nareyro. Although they were not living together, they did observe the Maasai way of family planning by spacing the children.

The biological father then made one more attempt to propose, announcing to them that they were his children! On receiving a negative answer once again, he then left his would-be father-in-law's homestead very unhappy, but went back there a few days later, bringing with him a baby boy doll (in Kimaasai *enkerai esargab*) carrying with him a bow and arrows, a calabash with grass tied around it (*ilperes*) as a sign of pleading with them to let him take his children's mother as he had not lost hope! On seeing this, the elders in Naini's father's village felt very sorry for him. As a settlement, her biological father then suggested to his younger brother to marry Naini's mother in order that she and her sister remained in the same family. Naturally once their mother was married she would always be with them in the same home.

This is Maasai diplomacy. The same would apply in a case whereby a brother dies – his brother would marry the widow in order to protect the offspring. Whether the two brothers are alive or not, the children will always call themselves sisters and brothers (in Kimaasai *inkanashera* or *ilalashera*) as opposed to the English people who call them uncles in the family reorganization. On the other hand, in Maasai land, uncles are from the mother's side and not the father's side. It was then he decided that he would not date Naini's mother any more as there was no use continuing when their parents could not give them their blessings. And that was not all. Now that he had found a solution for his problems he was happy. While Naini's sister remained with her grandparents, Naini was then taken to her adoptive father, who was actually her father, since he was the brother of her biological father! From then onwards, their adoptive father continued to bring them up.

As for the clay doll, each time Naini was given milk, her mother was advised to feed it too and to oil it for eight days so that it did not crack, as if it cracked, it would bring bad omens and she might never bear children again.

It was only after Naini's marriage with Tim that she learnt all this from her mother. She then wrote to her father about her daily disputes with Tim, and he acknowledged by writing her a letter. It is all she has left to remember him.

Naini and her sister had happy moments of playing together during their childhood, before being separated. Naini was then taken from village (a) which was her grandmother's to village (b), while her sister remained at the original homestead. Naini spent the rest of her youth attending school while staying at her younger father's home (brother of her father) – in Kimaasai *enkang' e papaai oti*. Although she changed homes several times to enable her to live near the school, her younger father remained her guide throughout that period and he always ensured that her welfare and upkeep was catered for. She never forgot the little nice things he did for her while she lived at his home.

Naini's sister was then left with their grandmother as customary since she was old, and did not get a chance to go to school. She lived with her until her youth, till she was nearing the time for circumcision. She then moved to their father's home so as to be circumcised. She underwent all the Maasai traditions, most of which Naini did not go through herself. What made Naini so different from her sister was that they were brought up in different ways and different surroundings, but despite this fact they got along together. Naini got a chance to go to school, even though not for a long time, while on the other hand her sister didn't. Naini had a hard childhood as well as a difficult past, while her sister's was happy. They loved one another, and always tried to help each other in small ways whenever possible. Nareyro was a great girl and Naini admired her intelligence and her style of working as she was very organized.

A long time ago, Nareyro asked Naini to give her some money so that she could buy a goat for her, which was actually 50 shillings by that time, and as the years went by, Naini completely forgot the money and her sister reminded her. Naini wasn't even remembering about the lone goat, but one day when she needed money, her sister told her that she had ten goats for her. What a surprise! Naini then sold the goats as she needed some money to help another relative and only left one. The other day, she also sold ten others from the same 50 shillings.

Had Nareyro not been a very honest person, she could have told Naini that they had died, which is what many people would tell you once they sell or slaughter your goat or sheep if you are so far away. She also assisted whenever possible their family members, including distant relatives.

Naini's sister seemed to be content with what was there, and her life – that of a traditional Maasai. While on Naini's side, she seemed to have revolted, perhaps because of the mixed cultures she was in. While she moved as one in a dream to try to adapt to the European way of life, at the same time she was determined to preserve her Maasai culture; this made life even harder.

After circumcision, Nareyro was then married to Ole Sambu, after being given away in the traditional ceremonies (*aelaa esiankiki*) on engagement and proper Maasai marriage. After living with her husband for a few months, she was blessed to get pregnant and gave birth to a healthy baby boy.

173

They all celebrated the arrival of the infant. During the pregnancy, her mother-in-law had advised her on what to eat and what not to eat, as customary. She got along with Naimutie, who was the second wife of Ole Sambu. That same wife had no children. During her third pregnancy, her husband and the co-wife, approached her to discuss the wish of Naimutie to adopt the unborn baby, and this was agreed between the three of them.

It was on one Wednesday morning just after sunrise that Nareyro gave birth to a healthy baby boy delivered by her grandmother! After cutting the *o-sotua le nkerai* (umbilical cord), Naini's sister's newborn baby boy was then told in Kimaasai, '*Imbung'a ol-tau lino mai-mbung'a o-lalai*' (literal translation: 'Hold your heart and I hold mine', but the meaning is 'You are now dependent on yourself as you no longer depend on my blood. Whatever happens from now on, I am not to blame'. In general, this is said by the biological mother in all cases even if the child is not being given for adoption.

So, after the birth of her third child, she then gave away the said baby for adoption to the co-wife Naimutie, a few minutes after delivery.

The newborn baby was then given a name (*oi-taari*) then the blessing was said, which went like this: '*Mikitamanya ina arna*', meaning, 'May that name live with you'.

Naini's sister had just finished uttering these words then soon after gave away the baby to Naimutie without breast-feeding the infant (*a-ishoyo en-kerai tol-togom*).

Naimutie had awaited the arrival of the baby with anticipation, and in turn gave Nareyro a heifer known as *en-kiteng e-nkitati*, which when translated means the cow of the belt. The type of belt referred to in this context is the wide special belt used by Maasai nursing women after delivery, but in this case, it is for her to tie her stomach in order to try to forget her child as if that child had died. As for the cow, it is for her to keep and this would build up their relationship. Nareyro had done this with the consent of their husband.

Ole Sambu was a very wise old man. He was also very understanding for having suggested the above to his two

174

wives as he cared for all of them and he did not want to divorce Naimutie for lack of not having children.

Nareyro then continued living with her husband and got five children in all. All her children went to school. Some are now working, married and have children. Nareyro is happy to be a grandmother, and so is Naini.

Their parents' relationship with Ole Sambu started long before he even married Nareyro. At first, Ole Sambu had to see their father with the intention of marrying Naini, but due to another proposal from Tim's family, he was told to wait for the younger sister (in Kimaasai *nejokini metaanyu siadi*, literal translation: wait for the one behind). This was how he married Naini's sister at last as a third wife.

When Nareyro arrived at Ole Sambu's home, she was welcomed by the family members, who in turn gave her domestic animals as customary to welcome her to her new home.

After the death of her husband, Nareyro and the other two wives, their children and grandchildren, all gathered for the last time to give a big ceremonial funeral to a great elder and the head of the home. His burial was also attended by many members of the clan as well as friends of the family from other parts of Maasai land and non-Maasai who lived across the border. Having been a market inspector for many years, he earned himself respect and acquired many friends. Ole Sambu also fought during the war in Burma as a young man.

13

DEATH AND THE MAASAI

When an elderly man is about to pass away (*aitanya*) or immediately after his death, a fat steer is to be slaughtered – *Nenyieng'i ol-kiteny osinya*, meaning an ox without blemishes believed to be pure is chosen for the anointment. Preferred colours are three only. *Olorok oi-bor oshoke*, or *Sirua* a light grey colour or *Ol-kiteng onyokie oibor oshoke*. If black, it must have a white stomach; red with a white stomach.

Once it is slaughtered, the marrow is removed from the leg and put in the mouth of the ailing or dead man. This indicates that he has eaten the meat of the slaughtered animal. For a dead man, all the fat is then removed and fried until it runs (in Kimaasai: *nesholuni eilata enkiyieu nepiki enkoti eton emololong nepali omeiropija neanyuni o-mei-julujulayu e-nkolong*). The fat is then kept in the calabash till afternoon, between one and three, when the shadow inclines to the East. The body is then brought to the sitting room for the final anointment with the holy fat from the calabash. The fat will be used to anoint the dead man before lowering him down to the grave or disposing the body to the bush for its final rest. The anointment is carried out by all the relatives of the dead man, starting from the first son to the youngest, then other male relatives, then from the first wife till the last female relative.

While this process is going on, the body will be lying on an old dried hide of a slaughtered healthy cow. Generally it is kept in the first wife's house, if she is alive, and if dead, the house of the second wife. Throughout the night the fire is kept burning.

176

The fat is then applied, starting from the forehead then to the chest then the palms of his hands (*i-ndapi oo i-nkaik o-lki-maita* to his feet, using hands or the leaves of the *il-misigiyio* tree.

After the anointment, the body is carried either to the grave or to the bush by two men. In olden days, the carrying of the body was done by poor men or homeless men (*ilmeek* or *il-kiriko*). If the family decides to bury their dead, the two men are to lower the body gently to its resting place, making sure that it is laid on the right-hand side, head pointing eastwards towards sunrise and the face customarily towards the right-hand side. This applies to both men and women. The most respected man is buried in the middle of the kraal or cattle-pen. The soil is then returned to the grave, beginning with the family members followed by other relatives and then the rest of his friends.

There is another way of disposing of the body after the ceremonies – leaving it at a sacred area under either *Olekunini, ol-nga'aboli* or was just left leaning on *ol-tarboi*. If the following day the body has not been eaten by the wild animals, then a goat is slaughtered and the meat roasted so as to attract hyenas. A left-handed person is left to stay until it is stiff then it is made to stand upright against a thorny tree, for example olodoridor.

The two men who carried the body, after the funeral will immediately go to the river to wash themselves for they are unclean before the community. They are not to talk to anybody until they are given *e-nkare pus* (literal translation: bluish-grey water, that is, milk mixed with water). After drinking *e-nkare pus* and after washing themselves, then they are declared clean. They are to be provided with a steer and a heifer for the work they have done. The one who held the head of the deceased takes the heifer and the other who held the legs a steer.

Shaving of the heads by the next of kin takes place the second morning after the funeral. From then onwards, people will visit the bereaved family to pay their condolences, bringing with them alcoholic drinks of various kinds. These visits take about a week.

In a month's time, another ceremony takes place, namely *e-nkielata oo i-masaa,* the anointment of the ornaments and the weapons of the deceased. Here again a fat steer believed to be healthy and without any spot is slaughtered (*ol-kiteng osinya*). The preferred colours are of *ol-kiteng sirua,* an ox of a light grey colour, *ol-barrikoi* a brown ox, or *ol-kiteng' Orok* a black ox. (In Maasai society black is a sacred colour in that it is the colour of the tribe inherited from the first man; when perplexed, the Maasai will exclaim: '*Ee Papa lai orok!*, 'O my black father!', in this way acknowledging God as father of the tribe and care for the tribe). *E-nkiyieu* is once again removed as before and then fried to remove the fat. The fat is then sprinkled on all the ornaments, weapons, tools and clothing, which are by then laid on a dried hide which was from a healthy slaughtered cow facing the East.

Disposal of the estate on polygamous marriage and other ceremonies is performed immediately after the funeral, and those performed a month later are such as the distribution of the deceased's personal effects etc.

At this stage, and after this last ceremony, all his belongings are then divided amongst his children and relatives. The distribution is usually done by the eldest brother of the deceased, assisted by another elder, or alternatively by two other respected elders chosen by the family in agreement with the clan. The men are the ones who will be in charge of the distribution ceremony of *imasaa* – weapons – after the blessing and sprinkling fat on these items, using *imbenek oo il-misigiyio* by dipping the leaves into the fat from the slaughtered cow, which is by now in a small calabash. One of the men oils the items, the other's duty is only to hand over to the person concerned. Before the distribution time, the elders note down what was owed by the dead man and any outstanding debt owed to him.

During the illness whereby the family sees that the man will die, the elders will call a gathering for the terminally sick old man to make an oral will and say if there are any assets owed to him and by whom and who should take what after his death (*ai-tianya*). This last phase is known as *ai-tujung'isho.*

During the distribution exercise, the elders, who have already ascertained how many *i-nkishu e-boo*, the heads of cattle that belong to the old man, are in each house, then distribute them in equal shares amongst the wives, with special emphasis on the number of unmarried sons in each house.

The eldest son is given a traditional stool plus a cow with a calf *en-kiteng' nalepo*. The said cow is chosen from the herd of cattle that belongs to the dead man. The second child, if a son, is given a sword. The third son a spear, the fourth a shield. This will continue until all the sons have been covered. The two elders will continue this process until all that was owned by the deceased, including clothes, is divided equally amongst the sons.

As for the girls, the eldest sister of the deceased is also given a cow as a token to wipe the tears (*neishori en-kiteng' oo il-kiyio*). All the other female relatives fall into this category.

It must be noted that, before the distribution of the deceased's belongings, his grave is blessed by pouring milk and native beer around it by his family members. The process is the same as the previous ceremonies, starting with the eldest son, etc.

After this ceremony, meat will be eaten by all the people present. Also alcohol and other drinks are provided.

After the man's death, his sons inherit (*a-jung*) his herds of cattle or his other belongings as indicated, irrespective of their ages. The eldest son of each widow will take charge of the cows until his brothers are of age to manage on their own. Generally the instructions left by a dying man are observed, as failure to abide by them will bring bad luck and will be a curse. In the case of a man having only one wife, the widow will keep everything until her children are grown-ups to divide among themselves. If any of the brothers of the late husband or in-law tries to interfere with her children's property, she has the right to call the clan and the chief to ask him to warn the man to stop molesting them and restrain him from interference of any kind. If the widow has no sons, she can in the future let one of her daughters stay at home after circumcision so as to bear children from whoever she likes.

After her death, her daughter's children will inherit the property. If they are still young, the mother will keep all the property until they are old enough to divide it amongst themselves, leaving a portion for herself. The ceremony to deter the widow from remarrying is *a-kolian*. Therefore, when the husband dies, the widow/s will undergo this ceremony of removing the *e-monyorit*, which is the marriage chain, from *in-conito oo i-nkiyiaa*, the beaded ear ornaments worn by married women in the lower ear rim, separating it from the string hanging between the ears, leaving only *i-surri*, which will then represent her children after the death of her husband.

Her head will also be shaved by the footpath at the same time as those of her children and relatives. The elders will also remove from the widow *en-kalulung'a*, which is a small iron ornament worn around the ankle, usually on the right leg, as well as cutting one corner of her traditional lower garment at the lower hem (*ol-choloi lo-lekesena*). From henceforth she will never wear that type of garment again until her death. The copper wire used as a small armlet will also be removed. The hand will then remain empty (in Kimaasai *a-isiu*).

This ceremony will indicate that they have been made widow/s for the rest of their lives. In general, this ceremony is undergone by older women, especially if they have grown-up children. If she is still young, and can still bear children, she will not undergo the ceremony. But if she has no children and does not want to remain in the deceased's home, she can leave and remarry out of that family; the dowry, if paid in full, should be returned. If young, she can remain under the care of the husband's half-brother so that the children can remain in the same family and the clan can assist them. On the other hand, she can still remain in the same homestead and not marry anybody and live there till her death.

14

FRANCE

Recently during the course of her duties, Naini met some French tourists who came to hire a car from the company she was working for. This was some time during the month of June. Naini immediately saluted them, then soon after the greetings offered them seats. J.B., who was going to be the hirer and signatory of the rental contract, sat directly in front of her on the other side of the long counter. Soon after that, J.B. pulled out his pipe and filled it with tobacco. While sitting there awaiting for the contract forms to be filled by Naini, J.B. started to smoke his pipe, breathing the smoke into his lungs and then puffing it out through his nose in and out, in and out. Naini immediately became attracted to him. She had watched him with admiration. For no reason at all, she was filled with joy. For no reason at all, she felt her body going numb with a deep desire for love. She wanted him as she had never wanted any man before. For some seconds, she was lost in her own world to the extent of forgetting the presence of her colleagues. She had imagined him kissing her and taking her into his arms.

When she came down to earth, she felt a bit embarrassed as she was trembling a little. The man too had noticed this, he told her long after that very first meeting.

During their discussion, while going through the administration process, it was nearly impossible to communicate. This was due to the language barrier as she did not speak French neither did they speak English.

During the course of their struggle to communicate, J.B.

produced a pocket French/English dictionary and pointed out to her the word credit ... she immediately understood that he wanted to pay by credit card. She then opened her side drawers to get a blank Visa form so as to imprint his credit card plate to have the details of who to bill afterwards. She inserted the estimated cost of hiring the vehicle for the whole period in use.

After imprinting the credit card, she called the Barclays Bank Visa Card International local agent for an approval code because the amount in question was higher than the contractual counter amount approved by the Visa Credit Card Company for services rented at any one time.

While we were still waiting for the bank to call back with authorization indicating the approval code for the amount in question, which was more than 10,000 shillings, J.B. began a conversation by addressing Naini directly. 'Why do you not speak France?' She realized that he had difficulties in pronouncing the word 'French'. Although his sentence was not properly phrased, at least she understood that he was asking her why she didn't speak the French language. Naini replied that she had never learnt it at school. At this juncture his friend Michel joined in, but his English was even worse than J.B.'s.

After a while the phone rang and the bank dictated the code. After Naini filled in the form and handed it over to J.B. for his signature. After signing, he gave it back to her.

Before handing over the car keys to him, on their way out from the office, he inquired if there were any schools that taught French. Naini answered in the affirmative but added that they were very expensive and that she could not afford them. As they reached the car, he extended an invitation to her to go and visit France. She thanked him but informed him that she could not afford to pay for her air fare.

Before going into the car, he once again searched her eyes, and as they shook hands he held hers in his for some time in silence as if their hands were glued together. They both longed for one another. They then exchanged addresses. He promised to write to her after his arrival in France. Then he also promised to leave the French/English pocket dictionary they had been using during their brief discussion, before leaving Kenya.

After their departure, Naini went back to the office. As soon as she sat down, her colleagues kept on teasing her for her blunt reaction. They were all very happy to see that at last her feelings had come back! They all encouraged her to keep writing to J.B. One young man who was there said, 'That was love at first sight.'

Another lady sitting next to Naini added, 'That was indeed true love.' Strange circumstances and situations make people look forward to seeing that same individual again, to search for more information about them so as to get close to them. On the other hand, sometimes when one meets somebody else one can hate him or her for no reason at all. Naini felt from that business meeting that she had developed a strong relationship.

And she was right. J.B. kept his promise. At the end of their trip in Kenya he left the dictionary at the J.K. Airport with one of her colleagues for her collection. When her colleague called her to announce this, Naini was very happy and promised herself that she would make use of the dictionary to the maximum so that if ever she met another French national, she would be able to carry on a conversation.

After receiving the dictionary, she sent J.B. a Kenyan postcard to thank him for it. However, she wrote it in English as she found it impossible to use the dictionary to write a letter.

After about two months, she received an invitation letter, and this was not all, J.B. had decided to pay for her return air ticket for a stay of 30 days. This invitation marked the beginning of her trip to Europe, which was going to be her new home for many years. As a consequence of that very trip Naini had to learn the French language to improve herself.

On receipt of the invitation, Naini immediately wrote back accepting the offer, and arranged for her mother to come over to Nairobi to stay with her children during her absence. The children had nearly finished their schooling. At the end of her first trip, Naini made up her mind to return to France, this time not for holidays but to study.

Having worked for the travel agency for many years, this was her opportunity to take the challenge to go and try her luck elsewhere. The idea of learning another language and going to Europe one day was conceived way back before meeting J.B. It was while Naini was still working in the travel industry that she felt the desire to venture further for her self-development. She had worked in a big town for several years, and was sorry to have to leave her homeland, relatives and friends at this juncture. But she assured herself that it was for her own betterment and for her well-being that she must go and study.

Naini then informed her employer of her intention to go to Europe to study the French language and perhaps live there. He could not believe it.

When she received her second ticket, she immediately gave her employer three months' notice. It was quite a hard decision to make but before the end of the three months, she had already made up her mind so she went back to tell him that she had fully decided to leave. Her employer was very sad that she was quitting her employment after serving for nearly 18 years, but despite this fact, he wished her a bright future. He then added, 'Naini, we shall leave your position open for one year in case you change your mind and wish to come back if the climatical conditions don't suit you.' Naini was deeply touched by this remark when she heard it. She thanked him and left his office nearly in tears. She then continued with her employment until the three months elapsed.

On her last day in the office, her former employer gave a farewell party for her. During that occasion, she was paid her dues in the form of a cheque. This included her pension for the years she had worked for them. Although it was not much, it at least helped her to settle a few of her bills here and there.

The next two weeks out of office were very, very busy for Naini. She felt as if the days and nights were getting shorter than usual. She was going over and over the details with her daughters about how to run the home and advising them on when and where to go for this and that and what was pending for them to follow up on her behalf, like house rent, electricity bills, water bills etc. This was because although her mother was going to stay with them, she would not know where to go and when they were due for payment since she could not read or write. Naini had to formalize all her travel documents, obtain the necessary visas and inoculations and get traveller's cheques from the banks concerned.

Finally all Naini's travel plans were completed. The day of travel arrived. Her children and other members of her family, including friends, escorted her to the Jomo Kenyatta International Airport. She then checked in at the Air France counter and requested a window seat in a non-smoking area. After obtaining her boarding pass, they all went to the airport cafeteria. She was feeling emotionally sad. One of her friends reassured her of her solidarity despite the distance that separated them. She said to Naini, 'Don't worry, my dear Naini. After all, your absence is temporary.' This Naini had taken seriously. This was yet another challenge which she had to meet in order to improve herself even more.

After a while the receptionist at the information desk announced that all passengers boarding the Air France flight to Paris via Marseille should proceed to the Departure Lounge. Saying goodbye to her family and friends, Naini had mixed feelings – sad and happy at the time. Happy that she was going to better herself but sad that she was leaving her family and friends. As she went through the immigration formalities to have her passport stamped, they all proceeded to the airport waving base. As Naini walked down the airport's main building stairs towards the plane, she could hear them calling after her. Although it was dark, and the waving base was dimly lighted, she looked upwards towards the direction where the voices were coming from and waved back to them. The space between the aerodrome building and the aeroplane was lighted by electricity, so that the people at the waving base could see the departing passengers clearly. Just before entering the aeroplane, Naini looked back once again for the last time in the direction of the waving base as, despite the distance that separated them, she was now on a much higher level than before. Then she entered the plane.

Inside the aeroplane, she asked the hostess to direct her to her seat after presentation of her boarding pass. Apparently her seat was in the economy class on the left row. Naini then kept her hand luggage in the hat rack above her head. Just before take-off, the stewardess went round distributing sweets, one per person. Naini requested a second one. They then demonstrated the precautions to be taken in case of an emergency, the use of slides through the exit doors in case of an evacuation, the oxygen masks and the parachute. Although this was the second time Naini had travelled by plane, this was going to be the longest flying trip that she had ever made – to leave her country, Kenya.

Just before departure at the J.K. Airport, the stewardess had told her to put the sweet into her mouth at take-off and suck it, but despite this, her eardrums got blocked because of the change of altitude. Two hours after take-off they were served with dinner as this was a night flight. Later that night, after being provided with blankets and earphones, they watched a late-night movie.

Despite what was happening in the plane and all the comfort, from time to time Naini's mind reflected back home to her inexperienced children who were now going to cater for themselves without her guidance. At the same time her thoughts wandered about, to imagine what her new environment would be like in the long run and what it had in store for her. Her employment was the only security that guaranteed her a regular income for her young family's welfare!

In the early morning hours, and still in the air, they were served with breakfast an hour or so before landing at their destination. Throughout the night, Naini had not closed her eyes. She kept awake in fear of passing Marignac Airport.

Just before the plane touched the ground, someone announced that they were now approaching Marseille-

Marignac Airport and read the weather forecast. A stewardess came up to advise Naini to fasten her safety belt. She showed her the warning lights with the words 'fasten seat belt' and the 'no smoking' sign.

The plane at last touched the ground and Naini proceeded to the airport terminal for immigration formalities. The plane by then was at the parking bay, so that the disembarking passengers did not have to walk in the open.

Naini walked into the airport building like one in a dream not knowing which direction to take. She got lost because nearly every word in the corridor was written in French. She remembered what her mother had told her many years ago and looked for a policeman and asked him for directions. After walking a few yards, she finally found one. She asked him the direction in the English language on how to get out of the airport building to the luggage-claim. In disbelief, he just stood there looking at her. She tried once again. This time he said '*Anglais* no!' Naini thought he said they do not want English-speaking people in France. She said in turn, '*Anglais* NO!' repeating what he had just said. Then he saw the horror on her face and took the trouble to speak to her.

Then Naini remembered that she had the French/English dictionary that she had been offered by J.B. in Nairobi some months before. She then opened it and searched for the word 'box'. She pointed it out to him while at the same time using sign language with her right hand to beat her chest to demonstrate to him. On reading the word '*la valise*', he pronounced it. To Naini this sounded something like *la vilii*! He, in turn, demonstrated to Naini using sign language by swaying his two middle fingers, between the thumb and the ring fingers of his right hand side in a curving motion back and forth. He was doing this to give her directions. The palm of his hand facing down to the ground, his thumb, ring finger, and the small finger all held inwardly towards the palm of his hand, his hand half bent in place of her two feet then he said, '*A gauche et à droite*'. To Naimi this sounded something like 'aguuoash e aduat'. Since she did not understand what the words meant, she looked at him and repeated the words once again, 'aguuash e aduat'! Realizing that she did not understand the last part, he once again demonstrated, swaying his arm to the left then to the right, then waited to see her reaction. Naini did the same thing while pronouncing the words in English. She thanked him then walked away.

Naini arrived at the French Immigration passport control desk, presented her passport and air ticket then waited. The officer examined her passport then looked at her then again to the passport, then stamped it. Soon after that he handed over the passport.

In the airport hall, Naini went to the Air France counter, for directions to the baggage claim. Here too the girl did not speak English. She could not even utter a word. She just stared at Naini and continued with what she was doing. Naini guessed she was very tired after working the night. After this she had no choice but to leave her alone. After walking a few yards towards the other side of the hall, trying to find it by herself, she fortunately saw the word 'baggage'. Unaware that she was supposed to read the flight details on the computer screen, as she was waiting for her box at the first conveyor belt, she saw it nearly disappearing into the main building behind some black curtains towards the direction it had come from! She ran as fast as she could to catch it.

After getting her box, Naini realized that other passengers were staring at her. Some were laughing. She became a laughing stock because of her ignorance. Although she felt out of place, she was not much bothered. She picked up her box then headed towards the airport's main hall, straight to one of the entrances and tried to open it. She pushed one part of the glass door but found it impossible to open. Then she tried the other part, thinking that particular one had a problem, but that one too could not open! She then accepted defeat.

Naini became frustrated as she felt that nothing was going the way she wanted. She moved away from the door. A black man walked past near her. By this time she was sitting on her box waiting for the family friends who were to pick her up at the airport. She spoke to the man in English, thinking that he might be of help to her, but before she could even complete her sentence, she heard him say, '*Je ne parle pas Anglais.*' Since she did not understand French, she thought he had said 'Papangile' – In Kiswahili, this could have meant '*baba Ngile*', that is, father of Ngile!

By now, Naini was getting impatient. She sat down once again, this time to decide what she was going to do next, if her host family failed to turn up. After contemplating for some time, she came up with what she thought was the solution to her problem. Since she could not speak French and the family were not there to meet her, the people could not help her and the doors were impossible to open, she would board the next plane and return to Nairobi!

As Naini lifted her head once again to check if she could find someone to help her, she saw a man pushing a trolley towards one of the doors at the hall, and this interested her and her mind became alert. As he approached the door, it automatically swung wide open. She rushed to catch up with him but before she could reach it the door had already shut. She had just missed it by inches. Thinking that it was the trolley that helped him to open the door, she looked for one then loaded it with all her luggage. But it did not open because when she came back pushing the trolley, she did not go to the door marked exit but to the one whose sign was marked entrance. Then she moved to the next door. This particular one was marked exit – and as she moved forward with her trolley, this time the door swung open. It was only then Naini realized that the doors were automatic.

As the door opened, she went outside the building to check if J.B. was outside, but re-entered quickly into the building, once again because it was still dark, secondly, because it was very, very cold.

To her relief, on re-entry, J.B. then appeared. After greetings in the French way, shoulder to shoulder while kissing thrice on the cheeks, J.B. said, 'Naini, I am surprised to see how you are dressed.' His English had since improved tremendously compared to the last time when she saw him in Nairobi. She in turn told him, 'Having come from a warm

189

climate, I did not know that it was winter, because there was no snow in Kenya except at the top of Mount Kenya.' This was during the month of November/December. They had not warned her about the kind of clothing she should bring along with her but at least she had carried a sweater. At the airport hall, she was then advised to dress more warmly before leaving the hall. She opened her suitcase, removed the sweater she had carried with her and wore it on top of her traditional attire.

Soon after that they walked out of the building across the road to the huge car park where J.B.'s car was parked. J.B. opened the car door for her. As she settled down inside, he was busy loading her luggage into the boot. After that, he went to pay for the parking. Naini could hardly see what he was doing because the outside of the car was covered by a mass of fallen snow. After paying for the parking fees, J.B. came into the car and sat on the left-hand side, then started the engine to warm the car before they could drive away.

At the last gate on their way out, J.B. inserted the ticket once into the gate pole and the ticket remained there, while the crossbar swung open and remained open until the whole body of the car, had gone through, then it dropped, shutting itself once again.

On their way, Naini told J.B. using computers to serve people is good and on the other hand, it is depriving people of employment! At that car park, three people could have been having jobs. He just smiled and added, 'This is development.'

The drive took them nearly an hour because of snow and the heavy traffic on the road. The large highways were full of cars heading in different direction in rows, stopping from time to time in observation of the traffic rules, at the traffic lights. On their way to the town of Aix-en-Provence, they stopped at Les Mille's shopping centre (Euro Marche) to buy a winter coat, winter boots and socks. Inside the car, Naini wore them to keep her feet warm.

On arriving at J.B.'s friends' house, Naini was relieved to find that the temperature was the same as it was at the airport hall. All the rooms were heated by use of gas, but despite all this her teeth were chattering. She was still feeling cold.

After lunch, they went for a drive to J.B.'s parents' home, which was about 100 kilometres from the first town. There, the weather conditions were worse but the people in the countryside used both firewood and electricity to warm their houses. So they sat around the fireplace.

The fireplace had a passage through which smoke escaped from the fire made of stones. For finishing, an outside surface was built protruding towards the sitting room that served as a counter, which the owner of the house used to display his hunting firearms for decoration.

Naini's first trip to France took her to many French towns, e.g. Arles, Pau, Payrennes at the French/Spanish border, Anglet, Biarritz, Nîmes, Bordeaux, Perpignan and Bayonne and many other small villages. For nearly a year, she always used the dictionary to communicate with the outside world. When going shopping, it was practically impossible to speak to anyone because all the items were labelled and kept on the shelves indicating their prices. At the cashier's desk everything was passed through a computer which in turn picked all the prices on the labels or codes. Finally, the amount one owed for the goods or foodstuff was indicated on the computer screen. There was practically no human communication. You paid according to the amount flashed on the screen! To Naini, this was a series of happenings. It was exciting and at the same time confusing, especially when it came to paying with coins. To be able to pay for something, Naini first calculated the amount into Kenya shillings to be able to see if it was expensive or not! This idea made it nearly impossible to buy anything. After some time, she had to condition her mind to think in French francs because there were many times she stayed without eating because she thought everything was very expensive.

She then thought if she was working in France, it would ease some of her worries. It was then that she thought seriously about how much of her precious time she had wasted not joining a school just after her arrival to learn French. This was due to her arrival after all the language schools had already started in October.

It was very boring to sit and not have much to do. Naini decided that she was not going to wait any longer without booking a place in school for herself for the following year otherwise she might miss a space. So she went to the post office to consult the telephone directories. She finally found one – Université de Lettre, Aix-en-Provence – then decided to write to them in English. They acknowledged her letter and sent her an application form and information on the requirements and fees and the dates of registration.

It was during one Tuesday morning that she found in the letterbox an advertisement from the French Women Association indicating that the association was open to all the women irrespective of their race or country. Then things took a dramatic change for the better and broke her boredom. Through this association, despite the language barrier, she established many good friends. Through this group, she was able to go to social gatherings, visited other towns and castles. During each visit, they most of the time made sure that during the discussion, whoever spoke English sat next to Naini to explain. Little by little she got confidence to speak the few words she had picked up from her French cassettes. Madame L.C. especially devoted her precious time to Naini during her school academic year to teach her how to pronounce the words correctly.

The months passed quickly. In August the following year she went for a month to attend an intensive course, while waiting to start classes for one year in October the same year. During her short course, she met many young foreign students; most of them had already studied French in their countries of origin for four years. Naini thought of herself as not so young, studying with teenagers who were fresh from school. This thought nearly discouraged her.

Naini reflected on where she came from, having quit her job to come to France, now unable to find a job because of the language problem. Then she realized that there was no going backwards, she must go ahead. Every morning she went to school for the whole day until 5 p.m. After school, on arriving home, she started to clean the house and cooking, and when the food was on the fire, she sat down to do her homework.

Finally, by the end of the third semester, she did her exams and obtained her diploma in the French language.

To commemorate her success, Naini gave a small party. The following day she began to explore every opportunity to find a job, in order to improve herself even more. She felt she was now ready to start a new life in Europe.

Naini then put in an application letter and enclosed her CV, then looked up the addresses of private companies which she thought might be interested in her services in the travel industry. Out of the three applications she sent, two called her for an interview. She attended the two interviews.

The first interview was one at a travel agency, which was more appropriate as it was going to be a continuation of what she was previously doing before she left Kenya. She felt proud to note that she was now competent in the French language. But luck was not with her. After a few days, she received a negative reply. Although she was not selected for the job, she had no regrets because her letter was in the first place amongst the short-listed from the many applicants. At least she got a chance to go to the office to be interviewed.

This was after two years of unemployment after terminating her previous employment in Kenya. The second interview, was at an embassy. Naini was selected for a job. She had to travel a long way for the interview but it was worth the trouble. After one month, she received a letter of appointment. After this new development, her heart was once again full of joy. It took her a few days to prepare herself to travel once again to Paris, this time to go and start work!

The following days passed very fast perhaps because of too

much anxiety. Then it was the next day they were going to leave for Paris.

The following morning, they woke up very early to be able to take the small train to Marseille to take a big fast train to Paris. On arrival in Paris, J.B. and Naini had to put up in a small hotel because the town was very expensive. That evening, after checking in at the hotel, J.B. went over and over with her the details on how to use the subway. Having travelled 800 kilometres that day, they retired to bed early just after dinner.

The following day, they went round in search of a room to rent but in vain. The major problem Naini encountered in Paris was accommodation. At one stage, she paid a housing agency 600 francs but never got a room because they claimed that the landlords chose to rent to tenants earning a certain amount of money. On their way to their hotel, by sheer luck, they met a lady who, after they explained to her their accommodation problem, agreed to lodge Naini for six months. They agreed on where to meet the following day in order to sign a document for their mutual agreement. Naini was to pay her a monthly rent of 2,000 francs! This amount was nearly half of what she was going to be earning. She had no choice, she took the offer. They moved in the following evening.

On their arrival at Marie's house, she showed them the room. After that Naini unpacked her few belongings and J.B. helped her to fix the plastic temporary wardrobe. After dinner they once again retired to their room. Inside the room, J.B. wrote on a piece of paper the directions for how to get to her new office. Side one of the paper read: 'From home to office'. He then indicated all the stations. As a sign for direction, he put an arrow – and for where she was supposed to alight in order to change trains, he drew a minus sign.

At last the day to start work arrived. J.B. and Naini left the house very early that morning so that he could escort her to her office. On arriving at her Metro station, she said goodbye to J.B. as she alighted. J.B. had to continue on the same train to Gare de Lyon, where he was going to take a train to return to the South of France to resume work.

After the departure of J.B. Naini was now on her own to learn her way around and to discover more about her new environment and to face the difficulties that may arise in any big city.

She arrived at the UNESCO building earlier than 9.00, the time she was to begin work. Since she did not know where the offices were, she sat in the lobby to wait for the officer who was going to be her immediate boss. He arrived just on time, and directed her up to the office. After a few minutes his former secretary arrived. She started the handing over, at the same time briefing Naini on procedures. They had a lot of pending work, so they stayed together the whole day. At lunchtime, they both went to the Economa restaurant, which was just within the building in Miollis. Her first day was very busy. It was during the UNESCO General Conference in July.

At the end of the day, Naini took the underground to the Gare de L'Est then came out to take the French Railways (SNCF) to go to Le Raincy, which was out of Paris.

Being unaccustomed to travelling in trains, Naini took a train going to La Rechelle, unaware that one has to watch out to be sure that the station where you are going to alight is indicated on the noticeboard at the station before boarding it. It stopped at Noisy Le Sec. After that it went through without stopping at the station she was supposed to alight at as per J.B.'s list! On realizing what had happened, Naini panicked as she did not know what she was going to do next. She just sat there while it continued moving. In the back of her mind, she thought that it was only one railway line, it would come back through the same direction after arriving at the terminal!

After passing two other stations, Naini decided to ask a couple who were seated next to her. They advised her to alight at the following station with them so that they could show her the platform for Paris. By the time she got the train back to Le Raincy, there were no more buses heading to her destination. That evening, she ended up taking a taxi.

On her arrival at where she was living, it was already 11.30 p.m. Paris time. She was feeling very tired and went straight to bed after taking a shower. She slept without eating because it was too late to start cooking, yet she was to wake up very early the next morning. She set her alarm clock for 6.00 a.m. so as to arrive at work at 9.00 a.m. She learnt her way around the hard way. In big cities, everybody is busy. People seem to have no time for others nor for themselves! She learnt to work like a robot. Always in a hurry! From that first experience of taking the wrong train, she learnt to observe the noticeboard. Since then, she has been working with the same employer in Paris.

Naini wrote to tell her friend Nick of her experiences in what she was currently doing for a living.

I like my present job very much. It entails mostly dealing with the public, which I enjoy very much as it is a continuation of my previous experiences in the public sector. It has always been my aim to create and maintain a courteous and friendly atmosphere within and for the outside world. To welcome them and provide information so that they may go and enjoy their stay. But most of all, to keep the country's name in the limelight. Having gone through the TACK telephone-selling course in the past organized by the post office in Kenya, I always try to maintain those standards. During that training, our teacher once told us that the telephone is a very important instrument, for contacting business, personal appointments, for government offices, for private institutions etc. He told us that the caller will know from one's voice what kind of person one is. This can be deduced from one's voice. Although the two individuals are far apart not seeing one another, that first greeting matters a lot. And I agree entirely with him. So in order to avoid any unpleasant outcome or strenuous relationship between the caller and the receiver, the receiver, must be prepared to serve the public with a lot of patience, because that public/audience can be very demanding at times. Although it is very difficult to please everybody, one must take insults as a matter of course.

196

To be able to do this, while at the same time maintaining efficiency, one must have information at one's fingertips, or if not know how to obtain it with the minimum delay possible. Most of all, one must always learn to remain calm and be tolerant despite the insults that may arise at times. A customer may have had a disappointment elsewhere and want to ease his annoyance by bullying, or want to wash his dirty linen by throwing his nasty words at the first human who comes his way at that particular moment.

It gives one a sense of self-satisfaction when the public utter a word/s of gratitude, e.g. 'have a good day' or 'thank you for your kindness/patience'.

Besides, people are my business. Every day, people call from all the various occupational groups imaginable to seek for information. The more I learn about other people in the day-to-day work and the questions they ask on matters related to my work and the answers – their ideas, interests, their points of view – the more it becomes interesting.

Due to the above points, this will improve my services for the next customer and my job performance, as I am not restricted in my social environment to the same nationalities which could produce boredom, dullness and dissatisfaction. There is always something new to learn!

These daily phone contacts have helped me quite a lot and will continue to help me become an expert in understanding people and the world in general. The day-to-day contact also improves the alertness of the mind. These daily discussions either over the counter or through the phone make me feel that I am making new friends indirectly through their satisfaction with my services. I owe a lot to my former employer as most of my professional experiences were gained through his guidance and the training I underwent, which have paid me dividends.

Naini went on to say she cherishes every bit of it, as she thinks without such exploration she could have never built strong grounds. Although, as a Maasai, she is quick at learning and with a quality of bravery like all the Maasai people, she added 'perhaps this is one of the qualities that has helped me to win through'. She goes on to say, in her youth and later life, she has always tried to select friends who are people with real potential and also associated herself with men of good quality, and she is still hoping to enlarge her social circle to a broader dimension with friends who genuinely want to see her succeed and who are full of encouragement towards her plans and think of positive things and ideals.

For it is wiser to cling to people who think progressively for one to move upwards with them. For it is better to be alone than in bad company of jealous people who want to see one stumble and be a failure as them, if they have not made it in life themselves. One may have education, but does not have respect. A quote the first American President, George Washington on self-respect. 'Associate yourself with men of good quality if you esteem your own Reputation, for it's Better to be alone Than in bad company. Be courteous to all, But intimate with few, And let those few be Well tried before you, Give them your confidence. True friendship is a Plant of slow growth, And must undergo and Withstand the shocks of Adversity before it is entitled to the appellation'.